MR. HOTSHOT CEO

KWAN SISTERS, BOOK 2

JACKIE LAU

Copyright © 2018 Jackie Lau. All Rights Reserved.

First edition: July 2018
ISBN: 978-1-989610-04-6

Editor: Latoya C. Smith, LCS Literary Services

Cover Design: Flirtation Designs

Cover photograph: Depositphotos

[1]
JULIAN

It's five o'clock on a Thursday, but I'm far from finished work. I rarely leave my office at Fong Investments before seven.

I pull up another report on my computer and stand up to stretch before I start reading. My shoulders are tight, and I can feel the beginnings of a headache.

Unfortunately, just as I sit back down, I hear yelling outside my office door.

"He's my son! I don't care what you say. I can see my son whenever I like. I know he's in there. Don't try to tell me he's gone home. He never leaves the office this early."

That's my mother.

"I'm an old woman. Eighty-nine. Could drop dead any moment. Show me respect."

And that's my grandmother. Po Po.

Oh, dear God. Both my mother and my grandmother have shown up at my office.

I feel bad for my assistant. Of course, part of Priya's job is dealing with crap so I don't have to, but it isn't her responsibility to deal with my family.

I swing open the door and see my mother, my grandmother, and a frazzled Priya.

Plus Vince, my brother, who is smirking behind them.

Shit. This is bad.

"I'm sorry, Julian," Priya says, wringing her hands. "I tried—"

"It's fine," I say. "You can go home now."

"What do you want me to tell this guy?" She gestures to a man in overalls, standing behind Vince.

"Who on earth is that?"

"He says he's here to change the locks on your office door."

"What the hell? I don't want the locks changed. Find out who called him and get him out of here."

"I save you trouble. Locksmith was my idea." Po Po lifts her head proudly. She's less than five feet tall and missing a couple of teeth…and she's a force to be reckoned with, especially when she has the support of my mother.

"Good call, Ma," my mother says. "Change the lock and don't give him the key."

Vince slaps me on the back before sauntering into my office.

"What's going on?" I shout. "What are you all doing here?"

My brother sits down in my chair, hands behind his head and feet up on the desk. "I'm just here for the entertainment." He's still smirking. That bastard.

"Wait a few minutes," Po Po says to the locksmith. "I have little talk with grandson, then you get to work."

The rest of my family parades into the room. Po Po sits down on the couch, and Mom and I remain standing. I shut the door, leaving Priya and the locksmith outside.

"*Now* will you tell me what's going on?" I ask.

"Look at the vein throbbing in his temple," Mom says to Po Po. "Not good. He's stressed. Gets angry too easily." Mom turns back to me and takes my hands in hers. "Julian, you work too hard."

"Of course I work hard," I say. "I have a company to run. You, of all people, should appreciate how difficult that is. You know what it was like for Dad."

She nods. "And then he had a heart attack."

That was three years ago. My father had planned to retire at sixty-five, but after the heart attack, he figured he'd better take it easy, so he handed control of the company over to me a little earlier than we'd planned. Now he spends his time golfing and traveling the world with my mother, both of them wearing ugly T-shirts and multi-colored fanny packs.

And this is the man who built Fong Investments from nothing and wore a suit every day.

"We're worried you will have a heart attack, too," Po Po says.

"I'm not going to have a heart attack. I'm young. I'm in excellent shape."

"I'm worried about your health in general," Mom says. "What if you burn out? That's why I want you to take two weeks off work."

I must be hearing things. "You want me to take two weeks off?"

"That's right. You need a break."

"It's not possible. I have too much to do."

"I've talked to Raymond." Raymond is one of the vice-presidents. "He said the next two weeks would be the best. Actually, it'll be more than two weeks, since you'll take tomorrow off, too. Eleven workdays and three whole weekends without any work. Seventeen days."

I look at my mother in horror.

Asian mothers aren't supposed to tell you that you're working too hard. They're supposed to tell you that you're not working hard enough.

"What am supposed to do for seventeen days without work?" I ask.

"You can relax," Vince says. "Like me."

"You've been relaxing for a full year."

"I know. It's wonderful."

I'm the oldest of three boys, and Vince is the youngest. He started a tech company soon after finishing university and sold it for a lot of money last year. Since then, he's been chilling in his swanky bachelor pad, eating and drinking like a king, jetting around the world, and chasing women.

I'm under the impression there have been a *lot* of women, but I try not to ask questions. I have a feeling I'm better off not knowing the details of my brother's life.

"It's only seventeen days," Mom says. "Seventeen days without coming into the office."

"Locksmith will change the lock so your key won't work," Po Po says. "See? Didn't I have great idea?"

Hmm. I can still work from home. This won't be too bad, actually.

"And you can't work from home," Vince says, holding up my laptop, tablet, and phone. "Because I'm going to put these in a safe for *safe* keeping."

I hurry across the room and try to yank the phone out of Vince's hand. He dodges me and rushes to the opposite corner.

"Aiyah!" Po Po says. "You act like little boys." She stands up and gets between us.

Dammit. I can't go after my brother when my grandmother is in the middle.

"You can read a book," Mom says. "Maybe go to a resort and hang out by the pool? Or go on a date?"

"Yes," Po Po says. "You work too hard, and now you're thirty-five, still single. All three of you in thirties, no one married, no great-grandchildren for me. Very sad. All my friends have many great-grandchildren, and I have none."

Her face scrunches up, and it looks like she's about to cry.

I suspect she's trying to manipulate me.

Mom pats her shoulder. "My friend Violet—do you remember her? She's two years younger than me, and she also has three children. She's already planned three weddings. Her fourth grandchild will be born next month. Four grandchildren, and I don't even have one."

"I do not owe you a wedding to plan and a grandchild to coddle," I say, gritting my teeth.

"But you do owe us two weeks away from the office. I won't take no for an answer. Raymond will be in charge, and your father can help out as needed."

"What does Dad think of your plan?"

"He thinks it's a great idea."

"Why isn't he here?"

Mom makes a face. "He's golfing again."

"You can't refuse," Po Po says. "If so, I will make your life miserable."

I have no doubt she could accomplish this.

"Every day at lunch," she continues, "I bring new woman to your office. Will say you're looking for nice bride. Also, will play Chinese opera music outside your door all day. Very loud."

Vince doubles over in laughter.

"Priya wouldn't let you do that," I say.

Priya must have been listening at the door because she chooses that moment to walk in. She's in her late twenties, and she's been my assistant since before I became CEO. She ought to be loyal to me.

Except apparently she isn't. Apparently, our many years of working together just mean she's comfortable saying whatever she wants to me.

"Your family is right," she says. "You work too much. You need some time off. If you come into the office anytime in the next two weeks, I'll get security to escort you out."

"You can't do that," I say.

She puts her hand on her hip. "Why not?"

"It's *my* company. You can't kick me out of my own company."

"I'm not kicking you out of your position. It's just two weeks, Julian. The company will survive without you for two weeks.

"Two weeks and three days," I mutter.

"I know you won't fire me," she says. "If security refuses to escort you out, I'll let your grandmother bring in these prospective brides and blast opera music. You need this. You can't keep working fourteen-hour days for the rest of your life."

I cross my arms over my chest. "Says who?"

It's my life. I can do whatever I want with it, and what I want is to turn Fong Investments into an even more successful company than it was under my father. My parents always had high expectations of us, and I want to make them proud. Plus, I'm the responsible son who gets things done. It's just what I do. It's unfair for them to expect that of me, then accuse me of working too much.

Besides, it's not like I don't keep myself in good health. I wake up at five every morning so I can work out in my gym before getting into the office at seven. Then I'll stay at work until about eight o'clock at night, go home and eat dinner, maybe read another report. After that, I'll watch a TV show.

See? I have free time. Not as much as Vince, but he has far too much of it.

I look toward him and he grins.

"I'll help you figure out what to do with your time," he says. "I'm going to a party tomorrow night. What do you say?"

When I was a university student, I once went to a crazy party, which ended with me puking and passing out. That was sixteen years ago, and I've never done anything like that again.

I suspect this is the sort of party Vince has in mind, not a fancy charity event where I can schmooze with important business people.

"Are you ready for me yet?" It's the locksmith. He's standing in the doorway.

"Almost done," Po Po says. "Just wait."

My mother, my grandmother, and my assistant stand before me with their arms crossed. It's a rather terrifying sight.

"You know you're screwed," Vince says. "When we're all on the same side, there's no stopping us. Remember, Dad's on our side, too, and I'm sure Cedric will be as well, once I tell him." Cedric is my other brother.

I sigh and scrub my hand over my face. "Fine. I'll take two weeks off work."

But here's my little secret: I don't actually intend to take the full two weeks off.

Instead, I'll stay away from the office tomorrow and Monday, and I won't come in on the weekend, either. Hopefully four days will be enough to appease them, and then they'll move on from this little Julian-is-banned-from-work decree.

Four days without work is bad enough, but seventeen days?

Not happening.

After having dinner at a Thai restaurant with Mom, Po Po, and Vince, I get home at seven thirty. I live in the penthouse of a condo building in downtown Toronto. It's only a ten-minute walk from Fong Investments, so it's very convenient.

With a groan, I collapse on the couch in the living room. Not because I'm exhausted—far from it. I'm home earlier than usual, in fact.

What on earth am I going to do for the next four days? I can barely comprehend the idea of having so much free time. I can't remember the last time this happened to me.

Probably when I was in kindergarten, if that. We always had lots of activities: baseball, soccer, piano, math class, Chinese school…

The thought of Chinese school reminds me that I'm teaching myself Spanish—I'm nearly fluent. For the next few days, I can immerse myself in Latin American literature and popular culture. Maybe I'll even binge-watch a TV show in Spanish. Apparently, binge-watching is when you watch several episodes back-to-back. I've never done it—when would I have the time?—but I could give it a try.

I'm about to pull out my phone to look for some new shows when I remember that Vince confiscated it.

Damn. It's going to be a *very* long four days.

[2]
COURTNEY

I ROCK HEATHER BACK and forth, careful to support her neck as she is only a month old.

Heather decides she's hungry and starts looking for a nipple. Unfortunately for her, I am her aunt, not her mother, and cannot provide her with the breast milk she seeks. Also, she's latching onto my shoulder, not my breast. She starts crying when she realizes no milk is coming from Aunt Courtney's shoulder.

I stand up and walk around the room, putting a bounce in my step, as this is what Heather likes. Or at least, it's what she liked the last time I saw her, which was four days ago.

"I asked Will if he wants children," says Naomi, my sister. She is Heather's other aunt, and she's sitting on the couch, watching me doing this strange bouncing walk.

"Oh? What did he say?" I ask.

"He says he wants one or two."

Naomi smiles. She and Will are sickeningly cute together, although Will would probably grumble about the word "cute" being used to describe him. They're in the early stages of their relationship, but Naomi says she "just knows," and to be honest, I feel that way about them, too. My younger sister and I have always been close, and this man is different. I can tell.

So now it's just me who's single. Jeremy, my older brother and Heather's father, is married, and Naomi is already talking about marriage and kids with her new boyfriend.

It's okay. I've always known it would turn out this way, and I'm happy for my sister.

Heather has stopped trying to get milk from my shoulder. She looks up at me with serious dark eyes, discovering her new world, and I can't help but smile at her.

"I'm Auntie Courtney," I say. "Your *favorite* aunt. Your *fun* aunt."

"Hey!" Naomi says. "Stop feeding her lies. Heather, don't listen to her."

Naomi looks at me and we laugh.

My sister was joking, but it's true. She's definitely the fun aunt.

Most people think of Naomi as a *fun* person, whereas I'm pretty sure nobody thinks of me that way. I have a PhD and I work as a biomedical researcher...things that certainly don't scream "fun." Plus, I'm the complete opposite of a party girl. Just the thought of me partying is worthy of another laugh.

It's a good sign that I'm still able to laugh, but that will change soon. It's August, and autumn is just around the corner.

It's been five years since the last time I was sick. I know it's coming, sometime this fall.

Because it's *always* five years.

Heather closes her eyes and starts sucking her fist. She's wearing an adorable dinosaur onesie. My chest squeezes.

You can't have this, I remind myself, and I try not to be sad about that. My life is pretty good. I shouldn't complain about the fact that having a partner and a baby doesn't seem possible for me, although I can't help longing for those things.

"You're just so cute," I say to my niece.

The front door opens. Jeremy and his wife, Lydia, have returned from their half-hour walk alone, which is a luxury for them now. Lydia immediately reaches for her daughter, and I hand Heather over.

"I think she's hungry," I say.

Jeremy and Lydia have been married for three years. I remember when Jeremy first brought her home, which must be at least six years ago now. I was in awe of her. She seemed like one of those perfectly dainty Asian women—completely unlike me, in other words—although that doesn't describe her personality.

It was actually Lydia's idea to set Naomi up with Will. Of course, what actually happened was much more complicated than a simple setup, and it involved a fake relationship, a long weekend at a beach house, and lots of donuts. It's like my sister is living in a damn romantic comedy.

I miss romantic comedies. They used to make so many of them, but now they seem few and far between. I haven't been to a movie theater in ages.

"Do you want to see a movie tomorrow night?" Naomi asks, as though reading my mind.

Like I said, we've always been close.

I shake my head. "I can't. I have to be at the lab until late to finish some experiments, and then I'll probably just go home. It's been a long week."

Naomi is not like me. She seems to have an endless reserve of energy, whereas my battery needs to be recharged on a regular basis. After spending the evening at Jeremy's, I won't feel like doing anything after my long day at work tomorrow.

Except drinking a gingerbread latte.

I smile at the thought of that latte. It will be well after five o'clock by the time I'm finished work tomorrow, so it'll have to be decaf. I used to think decaf lattes were stupid, but then I realized that caffeine isn't the main reason I have gingerbread lattes.

No, it's the short walk to my favorite coffee shop, eleven minutes from the lab, and the amazing aroma that hits my nose as I step in the door. It's the cozy couches and wooden furniture, the familiar faces, the barista who chats with me and makes pretty foam art. It's the taste of the latte, the spices. It's feeling naughty and special for having gingerbread lattes all year long, when usually you can only get them in December. (The gingerbread latte isn't on the menu now, but I'm a regular and they make it for me anyway.) It's a break from the rest of my life.

Yes, it costs five dollars, and since I have about three a week, this isn't a cheap habit. People complain about millennials wasting money on indulgences like lattes and avocado toast, and they say that's why we can't afford houses. But the real reason I can't buy a house is because houses are ridiculously expensive in Toronto and cutting out my gingerbread latte habit wouldn't make me hundreds of thousands of dollars richer.

It's five dollars that contributes to my happiness, so I consider it five dollars well spent. That's what I focus on in life—those little things that make the sun shine just a bit brighter.

However, at some point in the near future, I'll stop being able to appreciate such things. My niece might smile at me for the first time, and I won't feel anything.

There was a hint of it last week. I tried a new ice cream parlor and the ube ice cream was really good. Well, intellectually I knew it was good, but it didn't taste as amazing as it should have. It felt like I was experiencing the world through a thick blanket of fog again.

This week, I'm okay, enjoying my niece's big eyes and my gingerbread lattes, but I know. I just know.

It's coming.

It's inevitable.

∿

"How was the wedding?" Lydia asks Naomi at dinner. We're eating takeout from an Indian restaurant.

"It was great, except I discovered Will can't dance."

Lydia holds a sleeping Heather in one arm as she eats. "I never imagined him as an enthusiastic dancer."

We all chuckle at the thought of grumpy Will heating things up on the dance floor.

"But I figured he'd at least be able to slow dance," Lydia says. "It's not that hard."

"It is for him," Naomi says.

"Bad dancers are supposed to be bad in bed, but I assume he disproves that theory?"

Jeremy glares at his wife, though it's a fond sort of glare. I'm sure Lydia made that comment just to get under his skin. He's still not quite used to the fact that his best friend is dating his baby sister, but at least he's not totally against it now, which is an improvement.

"Any plans for the weekend?" Lydia asks me and Naomi.

"I'm going to a bachelorette party tomorrow," my sister says.

"Will there be strippers?" Lydia sounds quite excited by the possibility.

Jeremy glares at her again.

She rolls her eyes. "What? There were strippers at my bachelorette. It was awesome."

"I'm not sure of the details," Naomi says, reaching for the basmati rice. "Knowing the maid of honor, there probably will be."

"What about you?" Lydia asks me. "What are you doing, since you don't have a baby to look after? Going anywhere is such a production now." She kisses her daughter's forehead.

"Um." I don't know what to say. I'm not going to mention that I have plans to drink a gingerbread latte tomorrow and go for a long walk and eat gelato—alone—on Saturday, since that sounds pathetic. "We'll see."

In fact, I have no exciting plans at all for the next couple of months. Naomi and I are going to New York City this fall, in October or early November, but until then? Not so much.

~

The next morning, I get up at seven, as usual. It's already warm enough to eat outside, so I have breakfast on the balcony. I'm going to enjoy summer while it's here.

My balcony is another thing that brings me joy. For a few months of the year—no longer than that, not here in Canada—it's like having another room. I could have gotten a cheaper apartment in another building, but this one has a balcony, and it's near Broadview Station, which is only a short subway ride from the university. It's worth the extra expense.

Not only do I have a balcony, but it's a huge one. I have a comfortable lounge chair for reading, plus two other chairs and a small table. I don't know why I have multiple chairs, since I never have company out here, but I do.

I sip my coffee and look up at the sky. My apartment faces east, and the sun warms my face.

It's going to be a good day, I can just feel it.

After I finish breakfast, I head into work and get started on some experiments. I'm about to take a break for lunch when one of the post docs approaches me.

"Your sister's here," he says.

How odd. Naomi rarely visits me at work, but she works downtown, not all that far from me, so it isn't too inconvenient for her to come here.

I head out to meet my sister in the hallway, and she's missing her usual smile.

"My car broke down," she says. "I just got off the phone with the repair shop, and it's going to cost more to fix it than I initially thought." She frowns. "I can't go to New York. I don't have the money."

I feel a tightness in my chest.

Every five years, like clockwork, I get depressed. It started when I was sixteen, and it'll be coming back soon. It's hard to explain how, but I can already feel it coming.

Naomi and I had planned this trip to New York for when I was unwell. Of course, it wouldn't solve my depression, but it would give me something to look forward to—as much as I can look forward to anything when I'm struggling with depression. Getting out of my regular day-to-day life often helps when I'm feeling that way, too.

I was counting on that trip.

So much for thinking today was going to be a great day.

"I'm so sorry," she says.

She doesn't suggest I go by myself or find a friend to go with me. She knows that's not an option. I can't travel alone when I'm depressed; that's a disaster waiting to happen. It's not good for me to be alone for days at a time, and I need someone else to deal with the travel plans and maps because my brain turns to mush and the tiniest things seem like insurmountable problems.

And it has to be Naomi. She's my sister and best friend.

She's the only one who knows what to do with me when I'm unwell.

I consider whether I could pay for her share of the trip, too. I'm doing okay financially, and I can afford gingerbread lattes, but I'm hardly rich. Plus, I need to have a decent amount of savings in case I'm unable to work for a while due to my mental illness. Because I spent so many years in school, I haven't saved as much as I'd like.

I have to accept it. We're not going to New York. I can't justify the expense.

"That's okay," I say, not wanting to let on just how disappointed I am.

I had that trip to look forward to, but now, all I expect of this fall is a blur of heaviness and gray and sleepless nights.

Naomi squeezes my hand. "You'll be fine. I'll make sure of it, even though we can't do this trip. I'm really sorry. I just…I can't. And Will and I haven't been together long, and I don't want to ask him for money."

Since one car repair threw off my sister's budget, I'm a little worried about her financial situation, but I don't ask, not now.

"I just wanted to tell you in person," she says.

We talk for a few more minutes before she leaves and I head to lunch with a friend, my heart heavy.

After lunch, I return to my experiments. I've always liked science, always liked understanding how things work. It's incredible how much we can explain, isn't it? From the microscopic scale, out to the universe beyond our solar system. When I was in high school, I'd already figured that I would get a PhD and do research, though exactly which field, I had no idea. I found a number of things interesting. The fact that we can explain natural phenomena only makes them more amazing to me, not less, and science can do so much for us.

But when I try to lose myself in my work today, I'm not successful. I can't help thinking about the trip that won't happen, as well as my sister's finances.

At eight thirty, I pack up my bag. Some of the tension in my body drifts away as I head toward my regular coffee shop, one of my favorite places in the city. Still, I can't completely shake my disappointment.

If only a few thousand bucks would drop out of the sky and into my hands…

Even though I didn't set an alarm, I wake up at five o'clock on Friday morning.

In an attempt to fill some of my free time, I try to go back to sleep, but at five thirty, I'm still awake, so I get out of bed and start my usual routine. Working out, eating breakfast, reading the news. Vince has confiscated most of my electronics, but I still have my desktop at home, surprisingly enough. So I could, in fact, do some work if I wanted to.

Well, I'll save that for later, for when I'm really desperate.

I make myself another espresso and sit back in my recliner with a copy of *Like Water for Chocolate* in Spanish. *Como agua para chocolate*.

I'm still reading at nine o'clock when Elena, my housekeeper, comes in. She's about my mom's age, but unlike my mother, she has three grandchildren, whom she likes to talk about the rare times I see her. Most of the time, I'm at work when she's here.

"I can hardly believe my eyes!" she says, putting her hands to her cheeks and opening her mouth wide in an exaggerated expression of surprise. "You're home on a weekday!"

"Unfortunately, yes. Not by choice, I assure you."

"I know," she says. "Your mother told me all about her plan."

"You approve?"

"Of course I do. You work too hard. You need some time off."

Hmph. Everyone's on the same side but me. What's wrong with hard work?

"I'll make you something for lunch today," she says. "What would you like?"

"Whatever you want. We'll eat together, and you can tell me about your grandchildren."

I need to fill the time somehow.

By three o'clock in the afternoon, I've read more than half of *Como agua para chocolate* and watched two episodes of a telenovela. I've also eaten too much moussaka, talked to Elena for an hour, spent another hour in the gym, and tried to pull out most of my hair.

That's it. I'm going to the office. I'd planned to stay away until Tuesday, but I can't stand this any longer.

I put on a suit and embark on the ten-minute walk to Fong Investments. We have several floors in a building in the financial district. As I take the elevator up to the twenty-seventh floor, I can feel serenity seeping into my veins. Yes, this is where I belong.

I step out of the elevator and walk purposefully along the corridor. A couple people look at me strangely and elbow each other.

Priya immediately jumps up when I walk into her office, which is connected to mine.

"Julian, you're not supposed to be here."

"I beg to differ. I'm the president and CEO, and it's a workday."

Raymond enters her office. "I heard you were in."

Priya holds out her hand. "Ten dollars, please."

He sighs and deposits a ten-dollar bill in her hand.

"We had a bet," Priya explains to me. "I bet that you would show up at some point today, whereas Raymond thought you'd be able to make it a full day without coming into the office. But he was wrong." She smiles triumphantly.

Just then, I hear movement on the other side of my office door.

"Priya, who did you let into my office? Nobody should be in there but you and Raymond, and you two are out here."

The door opens. "Hello, Julian."

It's Vince.

"What the hell are you doing in my office?" I ask.

He shrugs. "Need to make sure things don't crumble to dust in your absence."

"I bet you're flirting with my employees."

He shrugs again, a smile on his face, then turns to Priya. "You owe me ten dollars."

Priya hands over Raymond's ten-dollar bill.

"What the hell?" I bellow. "I'm away for one day and this place turns into a gambling hall?"

"Just a friendly bet," Vince explains. "Priya and I both knew you wouldn't be able to stay away from the office today, but she thought you'd show up before noon. I, on the other hand, had a little more faith in you and trusted you wouldn't show up until this afternoon. And now, you and I will vacate the premises." He takes my arm and starts walking down the hall. Before we get on the elevator, he pulls out his phone and makes a call. "Hi, Mom… Yes, he did. Don't worry, I'll make sure he has fun tonight… Uh-huh… Okay, talk to you later."

Well, isn't this just lovely.

"How did you fill the first half of your day?" he asks when we're in the elevator.

"Television and—"

"It was Spanish television, wasn't it? Even on your day off, you tried to be productive by teaching yourself Spanish."

"What's wrong with that?"

"You need a hobby," he says.

"Learning languages is a hobby."

"You already speak five languages fluently. Isn't that enough?"

"What do you want me to do? Crocheting? Woodworking? Birdwatching?"

"Or videogames."

I frown. "That's a waste of time."

Vince puts his hands to his chest as though he's been shot.

"Cut the melodrama," I snap.

I swear, my blood pressure must be higher than it would be during a stressful day at the office.

By eight o'clock, I feel like my brain is rotting. I've spent the past few hours playing videogames at Vince's and eating pepperoni pizza. Admittedly, the videogames were not an entirely unpleasant experience, but I'm ready for something new.

Vince helps himself to another slice of pizza. "Remember I mentioned a party?"

"I don't think I'm dressed properly for the sort of party you'd take me to." I gesture to my suit. Yeah, I'm wearing a suit while playing videogames and eating pizza. I'm classy.

"Actually, that's perfect. It's a rather fancy party."

"Oh?" I'm intrigued. Maybe...

"Where there will be no opportunities for networking."

Damn.

"I mean it," he says. "Don't embarrass me by talking business."

Fifteen minutes later, we're in the back seat of a town car, heading to the Bridle Path, an upscale part of Toronto.

"Tell me about your friend who's hosting the party," I say.

"Brian Poon. His family owns some kind of big multinational company."

"Which company? And who does Brian have looking after his money?"

Vince gives me a look. "Can you pretend you don't run an investment firm just for an hour? Please?"

"I was joking."

"Yeah, sure you were."

"I didn't ask to go to this party, you know."

"But it's exactly what you need."

The driver approaches a grand house of gray stone with elaborate wrought-iron gates, which are open. He continues along the crescent-shaped driveway and stops in front of a fountain with a nearly-naked man and woman carved of marble. The garden is lush and has an abundance of flowers, and the entrance is framed by two-story columns.

We head to the door, and an Asian man in a blue suit answers. He smiles at Vince before turning to me. "You must be Julian. I'm Brian."

We shake hands.

"Tell me," he says, "is this your first orgy?"

[4]

JULIAN

I DRAG Vince back to the car and haul him inside.

"Could you excuse us for a minute?" I say to the driver, and he steps out. Then I turn to my brother. "You brought me to an *orgy*?"

"Look how tense you are," Vince says. "You need to get laid. Badly."

"I don't need help getting laid. I'm fine!"

"You're uptight."

"I'm *not* uptight!"

"Right. Of course. You're not uptight at all." Vince chuckles. "It's good to try new things, isn't it? They can make your brain think in different ways. Good for creativity. Good for business."

I stare at him. "You're saying an orgy might be good for my business? You've got to be kidding me. What if news of me being here gets out?"

"It's very discreet. Besides, you're a young, handsome CEO. You can pretty much do whatever you want. Nobody cares."

"Thanks for calling me handsome."

"Personally, I don't see it, but that's what people say."

I scrub my hands over my face. What a weird couple of days it's been.

"Even if I were interested in orgies," I say, "why would I go to one with my brother?"

"I just came to drop you off. Don't worry, there will be no family members present."

"No. My answer is still no."

Vince smirks. "How about this? You go to the orgy for at least an hour, and I'll return your phone. I'll call Brian to confirm you stayed and didn't just sneak out into the rosebushes. Unless, of course, you were getting a blowjob in the rosebushes."

"Too many thorns," I mutter.

Vince laughs.

The thing is, I do desperately want my phone back. A lot of my life is in that phone.

But this is not happening.

I don't consider myself a prude, but sex is something that happens between me and *one* woman. In private. Yes, it's been a while, but an orgy is not what I need.

"Let me tell you about Brian's sex parties," my brother says. "There are a couple dozen young, attractive men and women, everyone dressed up to make it classy. Hence the suit. Usually it's just people Brian knows personally, but I vouched for you."

"Thank you," I say with as much sarcasm as I can muster, which is quite a lot.

"I hacked into your doctor's computer system and got your latest STD test results to prove to Brian that you're clean."

I stare at my brother. He's a complete nut bar.

How did I end up with a brother like Vince? I'm a normal, hardworking guy, aren't I? How did my parents manage to produce both me *and* him?

"Look," I say. "I appreciate the thought. Except I don't, because this is crazy. I'm not going to an orgy so I can get my phone back."

I wonder if that sentence has ever been uttered in the history of the world before.

I doubt it.

Of course, I could get a new phone, but that's a hassle. I doubt my brother will insist on holding onto my phone for *that* long, though it appears I won't be getting it back tonight.

"Fine," Vince says. "Suit yourself. Now, there's a perfectly good orgy going on in there, and since my brother refuses to go, I'll take his place. You can have the car."

And with that, he exits the vehicle.

I don't feel like going home. I've already spent far too many hours at my penthouse today, so I ask the driver to take me to the independent coffee shop on Dundas, where I occasionally go in the middle of the workday if I need to clear my head.

I'm not sure whether Chris's Coffee Shop is actually owned by a guy named Chris, or whether it's just called that so they can have pictures of Chris Evans, Chris Pratt, Chris Hemsworth, and Chris Pine on the walls, plus a picture of Christopher Plummer on the door. I think it's silly, but they make good espresso and the second floor is always quiet.

I get my drink and proceed upstairs. There are only two other people here, and they're both wearing earphones and reading textbooks. I look out the window at the busy city and feel separate from it all.

I also feel guilty, like there are a ton of things I'm supposed to be doing instead of this. Except thanks to my family, I'm on a break from work, so this is exactly what I should be doing.

Okay, I concede they have a point. Just a teeny-tiny point. My parents value hard work, so if they think I'm working too much, there's probably something to that.

It's troubling that I feel lost without my phone and am struggling to spend a single day without work. Plus, I've been getting headaches regularly in the past few months, which is unusual for me, and my neck and shoulders almost always feel tense. I've been tired lately, too, and even when I'm exhausted, I often have trouble sleeping. Sometimes my heart beats quickly for no reason, and come to think of it, I've had a bunch of stomachaches as well.

Perhaps telling my family that I'm "perfectly healthy" was a bit of an exaggeration.

I'm sure if I looked up my symptoms online, I'd discover that I could have one of many awful diseases that would result in my imminent death. But I went to the doctor last month for a checkup and he said everything was fine, though it wouldn't hurt to decrease the stress in my life.

I look down at my hand, which is shaking on my espresso cup.

I've always worked hard, but that's been particularly true since I became CEO—a position I wasn't quite ready for—after my father's heart attack.

Hmm. Maybe I need more than four days off work. Maybe I should do exactly what my family wants. I have a company to run, but I can't run it if I burn out—which is starting to seem like a possibility—and there are competent people who can run things in my absence for two weeks. When I return to work, I'll be refreshed and ready to work hard, fourteen hours a day. I'll just try to avoid spending too much time with Vince, since he has a tendency to increase my blood pressure.

Yes, as frightening as it is to be away from the office for so long, I'm going to do this.

I take a pen out of my pocket and grab a napkin so I can start a list. Lists are always good. I like lists.

How to be unproductive in the next two weeks.

How to have fun so I don't go into the office out of desperation.

I cross these out almost as soon as I write them. The titles sound stupid.

Then it hits me that *having fun* is something I never think about. If I'm honest, it's not something I've thought a great deal about since the tender age of five. I'm the responsible one. I think about how to do things better and more efficiently. I think about how to make money. How to stay in shape. How to eat healthy when I'm traveling for business. How to do *more*.

But not how to simply relax and enjoy myself.

This isn't something you're supposed to have trouble doing. In my defense, Vince probably has enough fun for the both of us, but I can't let him blow me out of the water in this department.

I need a game plan.

Or does having a game plan to learn to relax sound completely ridiculous? Is it silly that I'm feeling some sibling rivalry here?

I am so out of my depth.

I ball up the napkin and throw it across the table.

There are footsteps on the stairs, and I suppress a groan. It'll probably be a group of people who will have a loud, annoying conversation about which Chris is the cutest or something equally inane.

But it isn't.

No, it's a single Asian woman, who takes a spot at the counter against the window.

I know this woman.

Well, not really. I call her Latte Lady. I come to Chris's Coffee Shop about twice a week, and occasionally I see her here.

Actually, to my embarrassment, I time my visits so I have the greatest chance of seeing her. Usually she comes at lunch time, around twelve thirty.

Now, though, we're both here at nine thirty on a Friday night.

I never order lattes. They're terribly inefficient. A straight espresso, with a little sugar if you absolutely need it, is best.

However, Latte Lady *really* loves her lattes. Not only does she always get a latte, but she smiles at her damn latte, as though she's happy to see it. She doesn't take pictures of the foam art to put on Instagram, as some people of my generation might do, but instead, she just enjoys it, her hands wrapped around the wide cup, no phone in sight.

I find this fascinating, I admit. I like seeing her.

It doesn't hurt that she's also quite attractive. She's a little younger than I am, maybe thirty, and her black hair is cut in something that I believe is called a bob. She often has a serious expression—she's not one of those perpetually cheerful types, whom I find obnoxious—but then she has that smile that just lights up her face, and that smile happens for something as simple as a latte.

A gingerbread latte. At least, that's what I heard her order the one time I was behind her in line, and I've held onto that scrap of information.

She puts her purse on the counter before setting down her drink. Then she stares at the foamed milk for a moment, as though it can tell her the mysteries of the universe, before bringing the cup to her lips and taking a sip. Her mouth curves into a smile as she sets the cup back on the saucer. She really does have the most beautiful smile.

I don't know Latte Lady, but I'm positive she would have no trouble filling the next sixteen days without going to the office.

To be fair, most people wouldn't have my problem, but something sets her apart from all those other people. *She's* the one who could probably spend a couple hours lying in a meadow, staring up at the clouds, and enjoy it.

Perhaps she's the answer to my problem. She knows how to get pleasure out of the simplest of things, whereas I do not. She has what I want, so maybe I could get her to teach me.

Who said I wasn't a creative problem-solver?

Well, my brother didn't say that, not precisely, but he

suggested that attending an orgy would be good for creativity and implied that was something I needed.

Screw him.

I'm quite fond of this idea, and since I'm a man of action, I immediately stand up and walk over to her, my half-finished espresso in my hand.

"I've seen you here a bunch of times," I say as an opening.

She looks at me and tilts her head to the side. She's wearing dark jeans and a simple black shirt with a wide neckline that nearly exposes her shoulders.

I feel overdressed.

And nervous. I'm going to ask a woman to teach me how to have fun, and that's not the sort of thing I'm accustomed to doing.

"Do you particularly like men named Chris?" I ask.

"Is this a lame pick-up line where you tell me that you, too, are named Chris?"

I bark out a laugh. "I assure you, that is not the case."

She looks at her latte. "I don't go to the movies very often these days, and although I know there are a bunch of young white male actors named Chris, I can't remember any of their last names."

"I'm Julian. Julian Fong," I tell her. "And I don't watch many movies, either." Usually, I'm far too busy to have time for movies.

"You're the guy who runs Fong Investments, aren't you?"

"That would be me."

"A CEO is trying to pick me up." She laughs. "That's never happened before."

"I'm not trying to pick you up. Well, not exactly."

Maybe I sort of am. As I said, she's very pretty. I imagine having her all to myself in my enormous bed...

I'm getting off track.

"I've noticed you," I say. "You always have a latte. But is it always a gingerbread latte? That, I'm not sure. I heard you order once."

"Always gingerbread. It's the best. Tonight, it's also decaf."

"Decaf." I make a face. "That defeats the purpose."

"Ah, but the primary purpose of my gingerbread lattes is not as a source of caffeine."

"What *is* the purpose?"

"They make me happy."

She states it so simply.

Yes. She is the right woman for this. She's exactly what I need.

She lifts up her cup and holds it up to my nose. "Doesn't it smell amazing?"

"It does." Admittedly, it's probably much more delicious than my espresso.

If I'm honest with myself, I don't particularly like the taste of a straight espresso; I just appreciate its efficiency. I consume a lot of caffeine to keep me going, and espressos are the most efficient way to do so.

Our fingers collide as she puts the cup down, and the contact of her skin against mine catches me off guard. I swallow.

"So, Julian Fong," she says, "what *do* you want with me?"

"I'm being forced to take two weeks off work," I begin.

"You are being forced," she repeats, "to take a vacation?"

"Yes. My family thinks I'm a workaholic in desperate need of some time away from the office. Initially, I figured I'd just take a few days off and hope that would get them off my back, but now I'm thinking I really do need a full two weeks. I've been stressed lately. Not sleeping well."

I'm not being efficient. I'm not getting right to the point. This isn't like me.

"But I have a problem," I say. "I don't know how to take a break. How to have fun. I ended up at the office again today because I didn't know what to do with myself."

She frowns. "I'm not sure I can help you. I'm not exactly a fun person, either. I have no plans this weekend, aside from going on a long walk to a gelateria in Leslieville. They make a delicious lemon cherry sour cream gelato. Welcome to my not-so-exciting life."

"You're perfect."

"No one's ever said that to me before."

"What's your name?"

"Courtney."

"Courtney, it would never occur to me to go for a long walk and have gelato." I pause. "You're planning to do this alone?"

She sighs. "Yes, I'm so cool that I was planning on doing this by myself."

Ah. She doesn't want to be alone. We'll be helping each other.

"This is what I want," I say. "For you to spend the next two weeks teaching me to enjoy the little things in life, a skill which I believe you have mastered and I know nothing about."

"You want me to be your manic pixie dream girl." She bursts into laughter. "You want *me.* To be your manic pixie dream girl."

"I have no idea what that is."

"Of course you don't. Because you don't watch movies and it has no relevance to your business career." She has a sip of her latte then sets down her cup. "It's a quirky, free-spirited girl whose only purpose is to teach an uptight man, such as yourself—"

"I'm not uptight," I say. For the second time this evening.

"—how to enjoy life."

She seems to find this a hardship, but I have lots of experience in convincing people to do things they don't want to do. Throwing money at a problem usually works wonders, and I don't think this will cost me all that much.

"How about this," I say. "I'll give you five thousand dollars for your troubles."

Julian Fong appears to be off his rocker. He's offering me five thousand dollars to help him enjoy his vacation from work?

Me, Courtney Kwan. The depressed girl.

I might not be depressed right now, but still.

I shake my head. I'm stereotyping myself. Some people think that those with depression are depressed because they don't appreciate life's little joys.

Not true. Definitely not true for me.

I'm great at appreciating things other people might gloss over, but every five years, it becomes impossible for me to do so. The colors and tastes of life just slip past me.

When I'm not depressed, though, I'm pretty good at it. Julian's not wrong. Actually, it's kind of remarkable he figured that out.

I've seen him at Chris's Coffee Shop before, getting a thimbleful of espresso. It's hard not to notice him, since he's always wearing these fancy suits that are tailored just perfectly. I don't know shit about designer suits, but I can still tell they're expensive.

In addition to his suits, there's something about him that commands attention. I'm not sure what it is, maybe…

Okay, I do know.

He's really fucking handsome.

So, yeah. Hot, well-dressed man in his thirties. I've noticed him before. I figured he worked in finance on Bay Street, but I hadn't realized he was *Julian Fong*.

His father is well-known in the Chinese community, the great-grandson of a Chinese railway worker, one of the few who managed to bring his family over from Toisan. Due to the prohibitively high head tax and later the exclusion act, this was nearly impossible. Early Chinatown was over ninety percent men, many with families back in China. But Julian's great-great-grandfather was some kind of business genius, and despite the vast amount of racism he must have faced, he managed to get rich enough to pay that stupid head tax and bring over his wife and children.

Then in the seventies, Julian's father, Charles Fong, started Fong Investments. The new immigrants from Hong Kong, who were generally wealthier than the earlier Toisanese immigrants and had money to invest, were more apt to trust him with their money than a white man who they worried would screw them over. But his clients were not restricted to Chinese-Canadians.

Charles Fong built a successful company, and he also founded the Toronto Chinese-Canadian Center, which provides social services to the Chinese community, including assistance to new immigrants and a seniors' home. He had a heart attack a few years ago, which prompted the Fong family to fund a new cardiology wing at East Markham Hospital. I remember hearing he'd handed control of Fong Investments over to his son Julian after the heart attack, but I didn't know much else about Julian.

Until now.

Actually, I still don't know much about him, except that he's a handsome workaholic who has made me a very bizarre proposal.

When he came to talk to me ten minutes ago, I experienced a sliver of nervousness. A strange man was approaching me in a coffee shop at night, and it was a bit weird. But my instincts told me it was okay.

I don't think my instincts were blinded by his good looks. They usually aren't.

Now that I know who he is, I'm more comfortable. I might not personally know his family, but still, I know of them.

Julian is looking at me, waiting for my response.

Five thousand dollars.

That's a lot of money for someone like me, though it's not a lot for someone like him.

I know exactly what I would do with it. Funny, I was wishing earlier that money would just drop out of the sky and into my hands, and it sort of has. With five thousand dollars, I could pay for Naomi to go to New York City with me, and I'd give her the rest of the money so she could afford any unexpected car repairs and other things that might come up. It would provide her with some financial security.

Whenever I make a decision, I consider what would be best for my mental health, and going to New York with my sister would be very good for my mental health. She'd have fun, too. Plus, she's the most important person in my life and I want to help her.

Although I'll have to spend time with Julian Fong to get the money, it shouldn't be too much of a hardship.

I take another look at him.

No, it wouldn't be a hardship at all.

Not that he's interested in me like *that*. The man could have nearly any woman he wanted, and I'm rather ordinary. So he's not really asking me to be his manic pixie dream girl, because those are always love interests. He's just asking me to teach him how to go for long walks and eat lemon cherry sour cream gelato, without the kissing.

Though I'd enjoy the kissing. It's been a long time since I've kissed someone, and that's entirely of my own doing. Relationships are not safe for me, as I've learned in the past.

It would be nice if I could do the kissing and sex business without a relationship, which is what Naomi did before she met Will. But I find sex very intimate, and I end up falling for the men I sleep with. Casual sex isn't possible for me.

"So?" Julian lifts his eyebrow, and that simple action causes a pleasant flutter in my stomach.

"Are you serious?" I'm pretty sure he is, though I'm having trouble wrapping my head around it. "Are you well? Do you want me to call someone for you?"

"My brother Vince is at an orgy, my brother Cedric is traveling the world and doing his version of *Eat, Pray, Love*, and my parents are at a charity gala. So, no, there is no one you can call for me."

"Your brother is at an orgy? You know this for a fact?"

"Yes, unfortunately, I do." He taps his foot impatiently. "So? Will you do it?"

"I need a few more details on how this is going to work. For starters, I have a job. Not exactly a nine-to-five job, but somewhat regular hours, in general." Except for today, because I had those experiments to finish up. "Unlike you, I can't just take a two-week vacation because I feel like it."

"Can I pay someone a lot of money for you to get the next two weeks off?"

I think he's serious. "That's really weird, and this is weird enough as it is."

He sighs. "What's your job?"

"I'm a biomedical researcher in a lab at U of T."

"Surely your lab could use some money."

"Julian! No. Like I said, super weird." I have a sip of my lukewarm latte. "How would this work? We'd meet up once a day and eat gelato or drink gingerbread lattes together?"

"Hmm." He drums his fingers on the counter. "No, when I do something, I do it right. Not just a half-hearted attempt."

"Okay…"

"I think you should live with me for the next two weeks."

I spit my latte all over him.

"Shit," I say, digging into my purse for a napkin.

"It's okay."

"Yeah, I bet you've got an entire walk-in closet full of suits at home."

"Something like that."

I hand him a napkin. "I'm sorry. I don't usually spit decaffeinated beverages all over people, but I thought you said you wanted me to live with you."

"You heard correctly." He pauses. "I believe I need serious help with this."

"What did you do today before you went into the office?"

"I got out of bed at five thirty and worked out. Talked to my housekeeper, read half a novel in Spanish, and watched a bunch of episodes of a telenovela. I'm teaching myself Spanish, you see. My brother accused me of trying to be productive. I guess what I want is to be productively unproductive instead."

"There's nothing wrong with using some of your two weeks off to learn Spanish. But you didn't try, I don't know, enjoying a beer on your balcony? I'm sure you have a balcony." His place is probably very swanky.

"Just sitting and drinking beer. And reading, perhaps?"

"Sure, if you feel like it." Sitting on the balcony with a novel and a drink is one of my favorite things to do, though my beverage of choice is wine rather than beer. Or a nice cup of tea. "But not a report for work. Not something that you need to read or that you're reading to improve yourself. A book you're reading for no reason other than that it sounds entertaining."

"What an odd thing to do." He's trying for sarcasm…I think.

Something occurs to me. "I thought you young, hotshot CEO types were supposed to be good at partying hard."

"That's my brother, not me."

"Which brother? The one attending the orgy?"

He nods. "Vince had a tech company. Sold it for a lot of money. The last year's been one big party for him."

"I see." His family is nothing like my own. I feel totally out of my league here.

"But I don't party," Julian says with a little wrinkle of his nose —which is rather cute. "And I have no interest in starting. I just want to be a little like you. Enjoying a latte at a coffee shop or a beer on the balcony."

I snort. *Nobody wants to be like me.*

He doesn't know enough about me to realize that, though. And it's true, I do have my strengths, but part of the reason it's easy for me to enjoy the little things is because sometimes my depression stops me from doing so. Thus, I appreciate it when I'm able to.

I don't tell him that.

"You don't party at all?" I say. "What about women? Seems to me the next two weeks would be a great time for, I don't know, lots of sex? Maybe not an orgy, but a fling?"

"It certainly did cross my mind when I invited you to stay with me."

My eyes widen. "I didn't mean a fling with *me*."

"Why not? Do you have a boyfriend? A husband?" He glances at my hand—I'm not wearing any rings.

"No." I ball up my hands, feeling self-conscious.

He smiles at me now, a different smile than before. This one is slow and sensual and makes my skin prickle with awareness.

Nobody has flirted with me in ages, but now Julian Fong is flirting with me. It appears he really does want me to be his manic pixie dream girl after all.

"I don't do casual flings," I say. "Not my cup of tea."

"What *is* your cup of tea?"

"Earl Grey."

His smile broadens. "I don't usually do casual flings, either, but there's a first time for everything."

"Too much commitment for you? Are you a one-night-stand kind of guy?"

"To be honest, I prefer relationships, but I'm terrible at them, so I don't bother anymore."

"Hmm. A young CEO who actually likes relationships."

"You have a rather specific idea of who I should be."

I shrug. "You fit a type. Sort of." I pause. "I don't do relationships, either."

"Excellent. A casual fling it is."

"I *just* told you that I don't do those."

Julian looks perplexed. He might not usually do casual flings or one-night stands, but I'm sure he has no trouble getting such things when he wants them. Even if he weren't attractive—although he totally is—he's rich and powerful, and that doesn't count for nothing.

"Besides," I say. "You've spent the last twenty minutes telling me that you don't know how to have fun. Why would I want to go to bed with you?"

Oh, God. Did I really just say that?

He steps closer to me. Only a tiny step, but it's enough to quicken my breath. He dips his head and whispers, "There's one place I *do* know how to have fun."

I'm thinking about it, and he knows it. His body pressing against mine...

"No," I say firmly. "Not happening."

He quirks an eyebrow. "You seem to find the idea appealing, though."

I do. However... "I'm not good at casual sex. I'm one of those women who get attached when they sleep with someone, and like I said, I don't do relationships." Too risky.

"Does that mean you never have sex?"

"I am not discussing my sex life with you."

"Very well," he says. "You don't want a fling, and I can take no for an answer. But what about the rest of my offer? Two weeks—actually, let me amend that. Sixteen days of helping me learn to enjoy my life and be productively unproductive, and you will get five thousand dollars."

"I'll stay at your place?"

"Yes. But not in my bed."

Did he really have to mention his bed?

"I have a guest room," he says. "You can stay there. I promise to behave myself."

It's strange to hear this man talk about behaving himself around me. By some miracle, he seems to genuinely find me attractive. Hard to believe.

Stop it, Courtney. I shouldn't think of myself as hideous. Really, I'm decent looking, and I can believe that men find me attractive. Just not men like Julian.

Julian, who has made this interesting offer.

I want to accept it. My gut tells me it's safe to do so and that I *should* do so. In the past, I've gotten into more trouble for ignoring my instincts than for listening to them, so I do my best to trust my instincts now, even if they don't always make sense.

I'll be able to pay for Naomi to go to New York with me, as well as give her some extra cash. I'll also have some company for the next two weeks.

I'm alone a lot of the time outside of work. Now, I'm an introvert and I do like being alone, but I yearn for a little more of a social life than what I have. When Friday afternoon rolls around and I have zero plans to socialize on the weekend, I start to feel twitchy. Being by myself can even be frightening at times, because when I'm alone for too long, my negative thoughts tend to spiral. It's not good for my mental health.

But if I accept this offer, I'll spend lots of time with Julian.

Although knowing he wants to take me to bed and being unable to act on that will be a bit difficult, I'm sure I can manage.

True, I hadn't spoken to him until today, and I haven't even looked him up on Facebook, but in a way, I feel like I already know him. It's partly because of his family's reputation in the community, but it's something more than that. I can't explain it.

I hold out my hand. He shakes it. His hand is warm, his grip firm—but not uncomfortably so—and oh my God, this is the first time I've gotten aroused from a handshake. A *handshake*.

"You've got a deal," I say, my voice trembling slightly.

Yeah, I can totally manage this.

Right?

WHEN WE STEP out of Chris's Coffee Shop, a sleek black car is waiting for us by the curb. It's only a short ride to Julian's building, which is on King Street, a little west of the Financial District. Excellent. Close enough that I'll be able to walk to work. It would suck if he lived far away, but he'd probably hire a car to drive me to and from work anyway, so it wouldn't be that much of a hassle.

It's a very tall building, and we take the elevator up to the top floor.

Because, of course, he lives in the penthouse.

When the elevator doors open, he places his hand on my lower back and guides me into his home, the simple contact drawing all my attention.

Until he flips on the lights and I see his penthouse.

I've been in nice houses before, but I've never been in anything quite like this. It's massive and mostly open plan, so I can see a lot of it at once, including the fancy stainless steel appliances in the kitchen and the enormous marble kitchen island. There are two sinks and tons of counter space; even that seems like a luxury to me.

I slip off my shoes and walk around. In the living room, there's a large white sectional couch, and I sit down with a little bounce. A white couch seems horribly impractical, but I suppose he can afford to hire a cleaner—or, hell, just buy a new couch—if he spills a three-hundred-dollar bottle of red wine on it.

Next to the sectional couch is a black leather recliner, and ooh, it's the most comfortable thing ever. Across the wall from the chair is an enormous screen.

"How many inches is that?" I ask.

Julian answers, but I don't properly register his response because the word "inches" has me thinking of something else.

Not happening, Courtney.

There are pieces of art scattered across his penthouse, although I suppose "scattered" isn't the right word. I'm sure they were carefully placed by his interior decorator—hell, maybe a team of interior decorators.

I wander around and gasp as I approach the window. It faces south, and I can see the lights glittering in the small piece of Toronto between King Street and the water, and then the Toronto Islands and the black expanse of Lake Ontario beyond.

"Oh my God," I say. "This is incredible."

I feel embarrassed for gushing over the view, but that's the sort of thing he wants me to do, isn't it? He likes the fact that I can appreciate the little things.

Though this is far from a little thing.

"Would you like to see the view to the north?" he asks.

"Yes, please!" I say, like an eager schoolgirl.

He guides me down the hallway and into a bedroom at the far end. The window encompasses one entire wall of the room. The view is incredible, all the lights of a city of millions of people. It makes me feel small and insignificant, but at the same time, I feel blessed that I have the chance to see the world like this.

I glance at Julian, who's staring out the window.

"I guess it's pretty incredible," he says. "But I'm used to it. I see it every day."

His gaze lands on me, and I feel a shiver down my spine.

"This is your bedroom." He gestures around the room. "You can see this view every day for the next two weeks."

The room is nearly as big as my entire apartment, and this is the *guest* room. I wonder how often he has guests here and whether there are multiple guest rooms.

I wonder what *his* bedroom looks like.

Don't go there.

In the middle of my new room is a king-sized bed with a soft grey duvet and a mountain of pillows. This seems too fussy for Julian, but then again, this isn't his room, and I bet he wasn't the one who set it up. There are a couple of pen-and-ink drawings on the walls and a comfy-looking black couch on the far side, as well as a television.

Julian hands me a remote. "If you want to watch television in bed, press this button." When he presses it, a second screen pops down in front of the bed.

I'm afraid I'm going to break something.

There are two doors in the room in addition to the one that leads to the hall. I poke my head in the first one and find a walk-in closet. Now, I'm not one of those women who's particularly excited by walk-in closets, but I can still appreciate a nice one.

However, it's nothing compared to what's behind the other door.

An en suite washroom with a Jacuzzi and a shower I've never seen the likes of before. There are multiple shower heads, and... My God, you could have some really great sex in here.

At that thought, I duck my head and turn back toward the bedroom. Unfortunately, I run smack into Julian, and for the first time, I get a sense of what's under that suit.

Muscle. Definitely lots of muscle.

"Um," I say, stepping back. "This is all very nice. Lovely.

Impressive. But…" God, he's distracting. It's hard for me to talk properly right now. "I'll need to return to my apartment soon to get my stuff—my clothes and other things."

"Of course. We can do that tomorrow morning. Until then, there are toothbrushes, toothpaste, floss, and other essentials in your washroom."

"What will I wear to bed?"

As soon as I utter those words, I clamp my hand over my mouth. I don't need to be thinking about that when he's in the room with me. I don't need *him* to be thinking about that.

I watch his Adam's apple bob as he swallows.

I wonder if he's going to make a comment about me sleeping in the nude.

He scratches the back of his neck. "I can lend you one of my T-shirts for the night."

Strange to think of Julian wearing something as basic as a T-shirt, but of course he doesn't wear suits 24/7.

I nod briskly. "Great. That works. Now, could you give me a few minutes alone so I can call my sister and tell her where I am?"

He exits the room without another word.

I sit down on the bed and take a moment to catch my breath. God, this is really happening. I'm spending the next two weeks in a luxury penthouse. Two weeks with this incredible view.

I pull out my phone and call Naomi.

She answers on the first ring. "Courtney, what's wrong?"

"Why do you think something's wrong?"

"Because you never call—you always text—and it's ten o'clock at night."

"Don't worry. Nothing's wrong. I'm just spending the night with a guy and thought I should give you his info in case anything happens." I provide his name and address.

"Julian Fong," Naomi says. "Why does that name sound familiar?"

"Fong Investments. He's Charles Fong's son, and he runs it now."

"You're sleeping with a CEO?"

I pull the phone away from my ear. "Could you take your voice down a notch? And we're not sleeping together."

"Then why on earth are you spending the night with him?"

"Actually, it's more than one night..." It takes me five minutes to explain the strange events that have led to this point.

"Right," Naomi says. "I see. Except I don't really see."

"I'm getting five thousand dollars for doing almost nothing. I'll give the money to you, and you'll be able to afford our trip to New York City this fall! Isn't that great?"

"Courtney, you don't need to get the money for me. If New York is that important to you, I can try to figure something out, okay?"

Nope, not happening. My sister will just put everything on her credit card, and credit card debt is the worst.

"It's no problem," I say. "I like Julian. This will be fine. And any money you don't use for the trip...you can keep it. A rainy-day fund in case you have to fix your car again."

Sometimes my relationship with my sister feels a little one-sided. Like, she's always the one helping me, not the other way around.

I really want to go to New York, but I also really want to do this for her.

"I promise," I say. "It's not a hardship."

"If you're sure... But don't stay if you ever feel unsafe, okay?"

"Okay."

"And if you're not enjoying yourself at all, you should leave, too." She chuckles. "I just Googled him, and I've decided you should definitely be sleeping with him. In fact, I'm looking at a picture of him shirtless—"

"Where is this picture?"

"It's in a charity calendar of half-dressed businessmen from a few years ago."

My excitement deflates. "Julian would never do something like that. I know him well enough to say that much." I pause. "You understand why I can't sleep with him, don't you?"

That road leads to inevitable heartbreak, and as I've proven in the past, I don't deal well with heartbreak.

When I was twenty-one, I had a boyfriend. Dane and I had been together for a year and a half, and I thought we'd get married one day. I was in what should have been my final year of undergrad, and I was excited about applying to grad school and figuring out what I wanted to do with my life.

Everything was going great.

Then I got depressed. I slid into this awful world where...I don't quite know how to describe it. You know frosted glass windows, like you might have in a washroom? It's like experiencing the entire world through one of those. You can't see it properly, can't experience it. My brain felt like it was full of straw, and my body felt like it was being weighed down by a ton of bricks. I could barely function—even getting out of bed and brushing my teeth was a ridiculous amount of effort—and the fact that I could barely function made me feel worse about myself, creating an awful loop of negative self-talk.

It wasn't my first episode of severe depression. However, it was the first time it had happened when I was legally an adult and not living with my parents, and it was easier to get help. I went to the health services center at the university, where I saw doctors, counselors, and psychologists. I did therapy, I tried a bunch of anti-depressants.

Nothing worked.

Dane was initially supportive, but he couldn't deal with me when I was depressed, not for long, and so he broke up with me.

Not surprisingly, this didn't improve my mental health. It got worse. I had to go on leave from university, and I spent a week in the hospital under suicide watch.

In other words, it nearly killed me.

I can't really blame Dane. If he didn't want to be with me, he shouldn't have had to wait until I was healthy to tell me that. But it taught me an important lesson.

In the end, I only have myself, and I can't count on a man to be there when I need him. I can't count on a man to put up with me when I'm in that state. Nobody, with the exception of my sister, can cope with me when I'm sick. So I haven't had a boyfriend since Dane, and that's not going to change.

"Sure, Julian and I are attracted to each other," I say, "but I can't afford to get attached to him, and if we sleep together…"

I've tried having sex just for fun. It's not like I've been completely celibate for the past ten years. However, I can't escape the fact that for me, sex *means* something. I wish I were different, but I'm not.

"You could end up dating," Naomi says.

"No. The risks involved in a romantic relationship are too great." Even if, by some miracle, there's a man out there who would stay with me when I'm at my lowest, it's not worth trying, not when failure means a risk of death. Plus, this is the worst possible time, since I know I'm going to slide into depression again soon.

So, I'm just going to spend time with Julian, nothing more. Make five thousand dollars for my sister and enjoy his lavish lifestyle for two weeks.

Naomi sighs. "You're too pessimistic."

"I only met the guy a few hours ago," I say. "It's too early for you to be matchmaking. Now, about that charity calendar. You were joking, weren't you?"

"Yeah. Julian isn't in the calendar, but his brother Vince is."

After I end the call, I find the photo of a half-dressed Vince

Fong online. He's a good-looking man who isn't lacking in abs, but he doesn't do much for me.

There's a knock at the door and I drop my phone, feeling embarrassed that I've been looking at semi-naked pictures of Julian's brother when I'm in Julian's penthouse. It feels like cheating, even though there's nothing going on between us.

"I have a T-shirt for you," Julian says. "Can I come in?"

"Yep!" I call out, turning the phone over on the bedside table, although I've already closed the browser.

He steps into the room and I suck in a breath, willing my heart to stop beating so fast. He hands me a black T-shirt with a V-neck.

Mm. That would look good on him. He could make an entire calendar of himself, wearing jeans and a black T-shirt, and I would buy it.

"Need anything else?" he asks.

"Uh, no," I say, feeling a little flustered. Thank God he can't read my mind. "I'm settling in just fine. Nothing else I need. Nope, nothing at all!"

He looks at me like I'm slightly deranged, then says, "What are the plans for tomorrow?"

"Plans? Um…" Then it comes to me. "Your problem is that you always need a plan, always need to know where things are going. You need to learn to be spontaneous."

"Spontaneous?" He says the word as though it's utterly distasteful.

"Yeah. You need to learn how to go with the flow and let someone else be in charge for a while. So even though I have some ideas, I'm not going to tell you what they are."

The truth is, I don't have any ideas. Hadn't gotten around to that part yet.

Julian seems to accept my words.

"Have a good night," he says before closing the door.

I breathe out a sigh and then change into his T-shirt. It's a little big on me, but only a little. I'm not an adorable petite woman who'd be swimming in her boyfriend's T-shirt.

Not, of course, that Julian will ever be my boyfriend.

But tonight I'm wearing his T-shirt, and it smells like laundry detergent with just a hint of *him*.

[7]
JULIAN

USUALLY I LET myself sleep in on Saturday mornings. Rather than five o'clock, I get up at six. But since I'm on vacation, I don't set an alarm.

I wake up at 6:02.

And I can't fall back to sleep.

Sighing, I head to the gym in my penthouse and do my usual workout. Then I have a shower, make myself some eggs and bacon, and sit at the table with my breakfast and a double espresso. I reach for my phone out of habit, but then I remember that my idiot brother confiscated my phone and refused to give it back because I didn't attend last night's orgy. So instead, I pick up *Como agua para chocolate* and read another chapter.

When I look at my watch, it's eight thirty. My God, Courtney is certainly sleeping in. I can't remember the last time I slept until eight. I pace back and forth. I want to get on with my day, but I can't do that until she's up.

There's a knock at my door

"It's Vince," says a muffled voice.

Great. Just what I need.

Reluctantly, I let my brother inside. He's wearing the same

clothes as last night, and he looks a little worse for wear. He sprawls out on my couch.

"To what do I owe this pleasure?" I ask, my tone of voice making it clear that I am not experiencing any pleasure whatsoever.

"Just thought I'd pop by and see what you were doing before I went home and slept."

"You haven't gone to bed yet?"

He shoots me a lazy grin. "Define 'going to bed.'"

So he came here straight from the orgy. How lovely.

"Are you drunk?" I ask. "On drugs?" What sort of drugs do people do at sex parties?

"Nothing serious you should know about."

"It's probably best I know as little about your life as possible."

"Probably true. What did you get up to last night?"

Oh, shit. Courtney is in the guestroom and could emerge at any minute and meet my wayward brother.

"Um," I say. "I went to a coffee shop, then came home and went to bed."

He looks at me in horror, his wide eyes a little red. I hope that's because it's eight thirty in the morning and he hasn't gone to bed yet, not because of aforementioned drugs that are "nothing serious."

"You," Vince says, "are no fun at all. You seem a bit twitchy, too."

"I'm just fine," I grind out. "I was enjoying a relaxing morning until you ruined my peace and quiet."

"That's what I do best."

"I'm well aware of that. Now, for the hassle of having to put up with you on this beautiful Saturday morning, could you please return my phone?"

I hold out my hand, and my brother regards it for a moment. Just when I think he's going to give my phone back, I hear an unwelcome voice. It's quite a pretty voice, but it's decidedly unwelcome at this moment.

"Julian, do you have a hairbrush? Or a comb?"

Fuck.

Fuck. Fuck. Fuck.

Courtney walks into the kitchen. She's wearing the jeans and T-shirt she wore yesterday, and they're a touch rumpled. Her hair is sticking up on the left side, but she looks lovely.

Vince's eyes practically bug out of his head, and then his lips curve into a smirk. He saunters toward her. "I'm Vince, Julian's better-looking brother."

She's momentarily caught off guard, but then she says, "I know. I saw the calendar."

He laughs. "Did you, now?"

"Hold on a second," I say. "What calendar?"

"The charity one," Vince says. "At least, I assume that's what she's talking about. To my knowledge, it's the only calendar I've appeared in."

I frown. "Why don't I remember this?"

"I didn't tell you about it. I figured you wouldn't approve of me getting half naked for a photoshoot, even if it was for charity. Like you said, it's probably best you don't know the details of my life."

Dear God. I have a headache.

"I think you were more than half naked," Courtney says.

"Mm," Vince says. "You're right." He turns to me. "You backed out of the orgy, but since you got laid last night, I think you deserve your phone back." He takes it out of his pocket.

I'm torn. I really want my phone, but at the same time, I don't want Vince to have the wrong impression. Yes, it looks like Courtney and I slept together, but we didn't. Instead, I made her a strange deal.

In the light of morning, that deal now seems particularly weird.

Courtney takes the decision out of my hands. "We didn't sleep together," she tells my brother. "I understand why you think that, but I assure you, it's not happening."

Admittedly, I'm a bit disappointed she's so firm about that.

"Instead," she continues, "Julian is paying me five thousand dollars to teach him how to enjoy life."

My idiot brother laughs his head off. "Dude," he says to me. "If you wanted to learn to have fun, I would have done it for free. Actually, I did my best to help you yesterday, but you weren't having any of it."

I cannot believe this man once ran a successful tech start-up and worked almost as much as I do.

"Look," I say, "I don't like your particular brand of fun, but maybe my family does have a point. I could use a break from working fourteen-hour days, and I need to learn how to enjoy myself."

"Huh. This is the first time you've ever admitted I'm a genius."

"That's not what I said."

"More or less."

"No…"

I trail off as Vince turns his attention to my overnight guest.

"What's your name?" he asks.

"Courtney."

"And you haven't actually slept with my brother?"

"That would be correct."

"But to help him learn to enjoy life, it's necessary for you to stay in his penthouse?"

"Apparently," she says. "He's under the impression he needs 'serious help'—his words, not mine—so I'm supposed to be around all the time. Except when I'm at work." Her gaze locks with mine and I swallow hard.

I really do want her.

I wonder if she actually thinks Vince is better looking than I am. That's an awful thought. God, what if he sleeps with her? He seems to sleep with everyone, and now he knows Courtney and I haven't been together.

This is a mess. I'm normally pretty good at cleaning up messes, and people depend on me to do just that, but I don't have much experience with this particular kind of situation.

"Let me give you some ideas," Vince says to Courtney. "Get him to smoke pot and send me a video of him while he's high. Or invite me over. I think my brother might actually be tolerable if he was high."

"Sorry to disappoint you," she says, "but I don't do drugs. Other than alcohol and caffeine, that is."

"Julian." Vince shakes his head. "I question your judgment. *This* is the woman who's supposed to teach you to have fun?"

"She's qualified. Trust me. And even if she tried to get me to smoke up, I would refuse. The only time I did weed—"

"You've done weed before?" Vince puts his hands to his mouth as though this is truly shocking, horrifying news. "Call the press!"

I glare at him. "It was fifteen years ago, when I was in university. It made me paranoid, which was no fun at all, so I've never done it again."

He nods and puts his hand to his chin, deep in thought. "The problem might have been the strain. Head to a dispensary and tell them you had issues with paranoia last time. They'll find you something appropriate."

"Vince," I say through gritted teeth. "Out. I'm supposed to be relaxing, and your presence is not good for my blood pressure."

"I'm aware of that," he says with a smile. "Nice to meet you, Courtney. Keep me updated on his progress, okay? And give him back his phone when you think he deserves it." He throws her my phone, and I watch in horror as it spins through the air. It's going to crash any second now and the screen will shatter—

But Courtney catches it in one hand.

Impressive.

Vince heads out the door, and I follow him into the hall.

"Don't you dare lay a hand on her," I hiss.

He holds up his hands. "Hey, now. You might not have sealed the deal yet, but she's yours. I understand that." He tilts his head. "A little possessive, are you? How'd you meet her?"

"At the coffee shop. She was drinking a gingerbread latte like it was the greatest thing on earth. She's the opposite of you, actually. You crave overstimulation, but she appreciates the small things."

A shadow crosses Vince's face, but it quickly disappears. Perhaps I imagined it.

"Well," he says, pressing the elevator button, "if you ever need tips on women, hit me up. I'll be out on the town, having a good time, though I think I should go home and sleep first."

"Yeah, you probably should," I say before heading back inside.

I sure hope the day improves from here.

[8]
COURTNEY

JULIAN STRIDES purposefully back inside the penthouse, as though he has some very important business to attend to. Two lines appear between his eyebrows and he frowns.

"I'm sorry," I say. "If I'd known your brother was here, I wouldn't have come out."

"It's fine. You had no way of knowing." He scrubs a hand over his face. "Unfortunately, Vince will probably inform my parents of your existence, and my family will descend on my home to meet you. They'll be thrilled." He does not say this sarcastically. No, he's serious. "They're desperate for me to 'settle down,' as they call it, even though my life is already pretty settled. My grandmother threatened to bring prospective brides to my office every day if I refused to take time off."

I laugh.

"It's not funny," he says. "Well, okay. I guess it's funny if it's happening to someone else."

I kind of like the idea of meeting his family. Since we're not actually together, I don't feel any pressure to get them to fall in love with me. Vince's visit was entertaining, and I think seeing Julian with the rest of his family could be entertaining, too.

"I could pretend to be your girlfriend," I say.

"Whatever for?"

"So they stop bugging you about finding a woman. Just for the next two weeks."

He shakes his head. "No fake relationships. That's ridiculous."

"I was totally against the idea of fake relationships, too. But then my sister asked my brother's best friend to pretend to be her boyfriend for a long weekend at a beach house, because she didn't want to show up by herself when her ex-boyfriend was there and—"

"My head hurts just thinking about that." Julian groans.

"Anyway, long story short, they're a happy couple now."

Crap. I've made it sound like I want a fake relationship because it could turn into something real.

I hurry to add, "Not that I want that to happen to you and me."

"Of course not," he murmurs. "What do you have against me, anyway?"

"Nothing. I just don't do relationships. You said you don't, either. Remember?"

He nods. "In my case, it's because I work too hard. I might want a relationship, but I'm too much of a workaholic for one to ever succeed."

"Is that what your ex-girlfriends said when they dumped you?"

"Yes. They complained that I was always at the office and wasn't emotionally invested in the relationship." He pauses. "But that can't be your reason for not dating."

"It isn't."

A silence.

"Care to elaborate?" he asks.

"Not really."

He seems to accept that. "Would you like me to make you a latte?"

"Ooh! Yes, please."

He smiles at me, as though he finds my excitement rather cute.

"I can't believe you have a fancy espresso machine," I say, then realize who I'm talking to. "Actually, I can totally believe it." I walk over to the counter and peer at the machine. "Cool."

"What would you like to eat?"

"What are you having?"

"I ate an hour and a half ago. Bacon and scrambled eggs. I can make you some?"

"Ooh, that sounds wonderful!"

He tilts his head and looks at me as though he can't quite figure me out. "Are you always like this?"

I remember decadent chocolates tasting like woodchips.

I remember my sister bringing me to the emergency room.

"No, I'm not. But this is an entirely different world for me, and it's kind of exciting." I hesitate. "Do you think I'm shallow?"

"Not at all."

I sit down at the table and watch him prepare my breakfast. I'd figured a man like Julian wouldn't even be able to boil water and would consider such tasks beneath him, but he moves around the kitchen with ease. It's been a long time since a man cooked a meal for me. Actually, I'm not sure it's ever happened before.

"Do you cook often?" I ask as he beats two eggs with chopsticks.

"Just on the weekends. My housekeeper makes my dinners during the week."

Of course he has a housekeeper.

Like I said, this is an entirely different world for me. It's like when you're traveling to a new city and everything feels brand new.

Julian is wearing jeans and a white T-shirt. I admire his arm muscles as he works the espresso machine, the perfect lines of his back. He exudes power, even when he's making a latte.

He doesn't look much like his brother, plus the way Vince carries himself is completely different. Vince swaggers or saunters into a room; Julian strides. Perhaps that's a silly distinction, but there's a massive difference simply in the way they walk. And sit. Julian would never sprawl on a couch the way Vince did. Julian's taller, too—he's about six feet, whereas Vince is maybe five-nine.

Vince also smiles easily, carelessly. Julian's default expression is more serious, but when he does smile, it's a zillion times better.

Actually, Vince looks a little different in real life than he did in the calendar. He's a bit lankier and not as muscled. Is that the camera or has his physique changed since that picture was taken a few years ago? I wonder if he still has a six-pack.

I expect Julian would not appreciate that line of questioning.

Julian sets a latte in front of me. "I'm sorry I don't know how to make a gingerbread latte."

I sip my drink. "It's delicious. Thank you."

He returns to the stove, and the smell of bacon wafts toward me. Few things smell as amazing as bacon in the frying pan.

"You have another brother, don't you?" I ask.

"Cedric is the middle child. He's a writer."

Right. I remember now. Cedric Fong's first novel came out a few years ago. It was a *Globe and Mail* and *New York Times* bestseller. I didn't read it because it was about a young, white, down-on-his-luck writer in Toronto, and it sounded...well, like the kind of thing that had been done many times before.

"He hasn't been able to write anything for a few years, though," Julian says. "He's currently traveling the world, trying to find himself and get over his writer's block, and...frankly, I'm not sure what else. I haven't heard from him in a while."

"My sister's boyfriend—"

"The poor guy who had to fake a relationship?"

"Yes. Will. He's a writer, too. Science fiction."

Julian comes over to the table and sets a plate of eggs, bacon, and toast in front of me.

"Dig in," he says.

I put a forkful of scrambled eggs cooked in bacon grease into my mouth and groan. "This is really good. You know, if the whole CEO thing doesn't work out, you could be a chef."

"Good Lord," he mutters. "I'm not sure I can be in your presence while you eat."

"What? Are my manners that awful? Am I chewing with my mouth open?"

"You sound like you're having a sexual awakening."

I stare at Julian. There's something intense about him, telling me that he never does anything in half measures. And, God, the muscles that are barely contained by his T-shirt...

I could easily have a sexual awakening with him.

Not happening, I tell my body. I can't afford to get attached, especially to someone who's admitted he doesn't get emotionally invested in relationships.

Definitely not happening.

I have a feeling I'll be telling myself that a lot over the next two weeks.

[9]
JULIAN

FIRST I HAD to listen to Courtney eat bacon as though she'd never tasted bacon before in her life, and now I have to listen to her shower.

She sings in the shower.

I have no idea what she's singing, and her voice is nothing special, but I find it cute nonetheless.

We're in her apartment. I'm sitting in the kitchen, drumming my fingers on the table as I wait for her to get ready and pack up. Then we're going to send the suitcase back with my driver and set out to do... I have no idea what. She's in charge and she still hasn't told me what we're doing today, which makes me a little uneasy. I don't like not knowing what the plans are, but I have entrusted Courtney to fill today with fun things and promised to "go with the flow," even if I nearly gagged as I said those words.

The shower stops, and I picture her pushing aside the shower curtain, wrapping a towel around her wet, naked body...

Damn.

I hear the whir of the hair dryer and wonder how much longer she's going to be. It's eleven o'clock and I still haven't really *done* anything today. Vince would be proud.

But when Courtney finally emerges, wearing dark jeans and a flowing red tank top, she looks so beautiful that I immediately decide the past thirty-one minutes—yes, I timed her—were worth it.

Her suitcase is white with butterfly silhouettes. I carry it downstairs and give it to my driver, and Courtney takes my hand, pulling me toward Broadview. It's strange holding hands with her, and just as I'm getting used to it, she lets go.

I start to ask her where we're headed, then clamp my mouth shut, knowing it'll be futile.

A few minutes later, I look to my left, expecting to see Courtney, but she's not there. Nor is she to my right. No, she's several meters behind me. I sigh and head back to her.

"You don't need to walk like you're late for a meeting," she says, slowing her pace even more. Then she spreads out her arms. "Enjoy the fresh air. Smell the roses."

"Right," I say. "This part of Broadview isn't particularly interesting."

A mother and two young children, maybe five or six years old, pass us from behind.

Nobody ever passes me when I'm walking. Usually I walk at a fast clip, and I want to punch the people who walk slowly and block my path.

But now I'm the slow walker. I ball up my hands in frustration. "I can't walk this slowly without wanting to punch myself."

She chuckles and slows down even more. We're barely moving forward at all.

I shouldn't have made that comment.

"Do you always walk like this?" I ask in horror.

In response, Courtney does something even more horrifying. She stops so she can answer my question. My God, she appears to be one of those people who can't walk and talk at the same time.

"Hmm." She puts her finger to her mouth. "Well, if you really want to know, I learned to walk when I was thirteen months old and then when I was two—"

"Courtney!"

She smiles. "I was just walking slowly to see how you'd react."

Damn her. But I can't help returning her smile.

She starts moving again, at a reasonable pace this time. Not as fast as I would normally walk, but it's a perfectly acceptable pace that doesn't make me want to punch things.

I let her walk in front of me so I can stare at her ass. I might actually enjoy walking at a turtle's pace if I always had this view.

We're sitting on the grass in Riverdale Park East, looking at the skyline of downtown Toronto to the southwest. I can see the office building where I would normally be at this time of day, even on a Saturday. I've never viewed the city from this angle before, and it's rather nice. At the bottom of the hill, children are playing soccer and baseball.

Courtney lies back and pats the grass beside her. "Join me. We can find shapes in the clouds."

I awkwardly lie back and stare at the sky. This doesn't feel natural.

I wonder how the office is doing without me. Do they know why I'm gone? What has Priya told everyone? Are they slacking off because the boss isn't there? And most importantly, how can I convince Courtney to give me my phone so I can check my work email? It's not like I'm going to do actual work. I just want to check my email.

She takes out my phone and snaps a picture of me lying on my back, staring up at the sky and muttering a curse word under my breath.

"I'm sending the picture to Vince," she says. "And to myself.

You know what we should do? Make a scrapbook of your two-week holiday. Yes! We can take a scrapbooking class together."

"I am not taking a scrapbooking class."

"Well, since you're stinking rich, you could hire a private instructor."

Dear Lord. Courtney better not meet the rest of my family. I'm terrified of the plans they'd come up with.

"Do people even scrapbook anymore?" I ask. "Don't they just make photo books online?"

She shrugs. "Dunno. I don't make scrapbooks, but that doesn't mean nobody else does. We could learn! Together!"

"No scrapbooking."

What do single men my age usually do for fun? Watch sports and drink beer and play videogames, I assume. But instead, I asked a woman to teach me how to have fun because…

Well, it's pretty obvious why I asked this particular woman.

Single men in their thirties probably also spend a lot of time figuring out how to have sex. Since Courtney declined my advances last night, I won't push it, although the idea is definitely appealing. I have a strong urge to roll on top of her and kiss her to prevent further talk about scrapbooking, of all things.

My phone beeps, and Courtney looks at the message and smiles. I bet it's from Vince.

No, no, no. I do not like the idea of my brother making her smile, even if he's promised not to touch her. I grab the phone out of her hand.

She giggles and reaches for it, but my arms are longer than hers, and I manage to keep it out of her reach, then put it in my pocket.

She climbs on top of me. I'm still lying on my back, but I'm sure as shit not trying to find shapes in the clouds, not when a woman in straddling me. When she reaches for the phone again, I clamp a hand over my pocket before she can get there. I look up into her dark brown eyes. Even if I couldn't see her pretty mouth, I'd be able to tell she was smiling from her eyes.

"Gotcha!"

Dammit. She grabbed the phone out of my pocket while I was distracted by her beauty.

I'm afraid this is going to be a recurring problem.

Also, she's soon going to notice that I'm aroused.

I sigh. "Fine. I'll let you keep my phone for now." I pick her up and put her on the ground. "But tell me what Vince said."

"Just 'Keep up the good work!' Don't worry, he wasn't flirting with me."

"Were you flirting with me when you climbed on top of me?" I can't help myself.

And I can't help but be pleased when she exhales unsteadily.

"No." She tucks a lock of hair behind her ear. "It was just the most efficient way to get your phone back, that's all."

Yeah, sure it was.

At Broadview and Gerrard, there's a small collection of Chinese restaurants and stores called Chinatown East, not to be confused with "regular" Chinatown on Spadina, or the Chinese plazas in Markham, Richmond Hill, and Mississauga. I haven't been here in years.

Courtney heads into a Chinese bakery with cheerful red décor.

"What do you want?" she asks.

I'm about to shrug and say I don't need anything, but then something catches my eye.

"A pineapple bun." I can't remember the last time I had one.

She smiles at me and takes two out of the bin with a pair of tongs.

"I'll pay for them," I say, heading to the counter. I'm going to pay for everything this weekend and spoil her with things she might otherwise be unable to afford.

Pineapple buns, however, are something she could afford. It's only a dollar fifty for two.

We sit down at one of the few tables in the bakery, and I bite into my bun and savor the crunchy, sweet topping. I loved these things when I was a child, and it tastes just as good as I remember.

"You know when I learned that pineapple buns don't contain pineapple?" she says. "Just last year."

"Really? They don't taste like pineapple at all." The topping just looks like pineapple, hence the name.

"But I figured there *had* to be pineapple. I thought I could detect a hint of it." She shakes her head. "My mind was blown when I discovered the truth. I felt misled."

I laugh and take another bite. "When my mother's parents came over from China, they opened a bakery on Elizabeth Street, and then when most of Chinatown was bulldozed—"

"Huh?"

"Chinatown used to be centered on Elizabeth Street, but when it was destroyed to make way for City Hall, some of the businesses moved west to Spadina."

"I didn't know that. I thought it was always on Spadina."

I shake my head. "Later, my grandparents had a bakery on Spadina, but they sold it when I was young." I have vague memories of going there as a child. Memories of my mother arguing with my grandmother in Toisanese because my grandmother had fed me too many barbecue pork buns, and I wasn't going to be hungry for dinner. I smile.

Courtney starts licking the crumbs off her fingers. I stare at her mouth, pineapple bun forgotten, imagining her licking the crumbs off *my* fingers instead, or better yet...

"Oh my God," she says. "Julian Fong, you have a dreamy look on your face. What are you thinking about?"

Uh, sex?

But I don't say that. I just take another bite of my pineapple bun.

And Courtney, goddammit, takes a photo of me while I'm shoving the bun into my mouth and trying to forget about the image of her licking things.

"Another picture for your scrapbook!" she says.

Twenty minutes later, we're standing in a store that specializes in cacti and succulents. Courtney finds it fascinating, and I'm trying my best to see it through her eyes.

And failing.

"Isn't it cool how these plants adapted to live in such harsh environments?" she says. I suppose this is the scientist in her. "You should get a cactus."

"I do not need a cactus."

"You don't have a single plant in that ginormous penthouse of yours. You should have something to brighten it up."

"A cactus is going to brighten it up?"

"You need a living thing in your sterile home, and a cactus is perfect because it doesn't require much attention. Just very occasional watering. You can manage that much, can't you?"

"I'll tell my housekeeper to take care of it."

She rolls her eyes before stepping away from me and walking around a table of cacti, presumably trying to decide which one would suit me the best.

"I always wanted a terrarium," she says, "but I think we'll just get you a single cactus." She bursts into laughter as she picks up a pot with a cactus that's about six inches tall.

"What's so funny?"

"Doesn't it make you think of…"

"I have no idea what you're talking about."

But as soon as I say it, I realize what she means. The cactus has two small protrusions—I don't know what else to call them— near its base, and it's approximately the length and diameter of, well, an erect penis.

An erect penis with spikes.

"Really?" she says. "You have no idea—"

"I figured it out."

"I'm buying it for you. I shall call it Joey."

"Why Joey?"

"Dunno. Just looks like a Joey to me."

That makes no sense. "I will not let you buy me a phallic cactus named Joey."

Well, there's a sentence I never thought I'd say in my life.

"Come on," she says. "I'm supposed to be teaching you how to have fun."

"Owning a cactus is fun?"

"I think so. Especially a cactus that looks like this. It'll be a great conversation starter, don't you think?"

"First of all," I say, "if I get a cactus, I'm putting it in my home office or bedroom, where I do not have any guests."

"Really? You don't have any guests in your bedroom?"

Not in a while, no. It would be a different story if Courtney had decided she wanted to have fun with me in the only way I know how to have fun.

Her face is turning a delightful shade of pink now, and oh, I want her to look like that because she's underneath me and my fingers are slipping inside her.

The air in the store is suddenly very hot—the sort of environment a cactus would like.

I swallow. "Second of all, I won't let you pay for anything this weekend. If anyone's buying a phallic cactus, it's me."

She brightens. "So you'll get the cactus?"

"If you insist."

Dear God, I don't know how I'm going to survive the next two weeks.

I walk to the cash register and the woman behind the counter tilts her head and studies me. "You look familiar. Wait... I know. You're Julian Fong, aren't you?"

Yeah, somebody recognized me while I was buying Joey the Phallic Cactus.

~

We're in Leslieville now, walking down Queen Street, and I'm carrying a cactus.

"Let's go to my favorite gelato place," Courtney says.

"We can't have gelato. We already had pineapple buns. That's enough dessert for today."

"There's nothing wrong with having two treats a day every now and then. Do you always live by such rigid rules?"

"Yes. Yes, I do." I shake my head. "Which is why I need your help. So, sure, we can have gelato." Even though it feels wrong, but then again, buying a phallic cactus also felt wrong, and I've already done that and the world hasn't ended. Not quite.

"You'll love this place. It's the best."

The sidewalk is suddenly crowded with people waiting in line for something. To my distress, Courtney leads us to the end of the long line.

"This is the gelateria?" I ask.

"Yep. The line-up's a little better than I thought it would be."

Is she serious?

"I'm not waiting in line for half an hour for gelato." The idea makes my skin crawl. I hate line-ups. They're such a waste of time.

"It'll be less than half an hour, I promise. They're quite efficient."

"They better be," I mutter.

"Are your arms tired from carrying Joey?"

"Mommy," says the little boy standing in front of us, "why did that woman say my name? Should I talk to her? But you told me never to talk to strangers."

Courtney doubles over with laughter, and I can't help but be glad she's laughing.

"I'm fine," I say. "The cactus isn't heavy."

"I'm going to scope out the flavors. They rotate. I hope they have lemon cherry sour cream today." She heads down the line and into the store.

When she disappears from view, I turn my attention to my new cactus and compare his dimensions to my own before realizing how pathetic this is.

Courtney returns. "You're in luck! They have it. It's the best thing in the whole world."

Admittedly, I'm rather curious about the gelato, though it's a pity I'll have to wait in line with a bunch of kids before I can get some.

She pulls my phone out of her pocket.

"I'll give it back to you in a moment," she says, "after I take a picture of you and Joey."

"Mommy, who's taking a picture of me?" Joey the Kid asks.

"The lady's talking about another person named Joey," the mom says. "Don't worry."

I'm about to open my mouth to explain that Joey is actually a cactus, not a person, then quickly think better of it. I force a smile for Courtney as she holds up my phone and snaps a couple photos.

"Perfect." She clicks a few things before finally returning my phone. A close-up of Joey is now the background picture, and she's sent a picture of me and the cactus to Vince.

Vince replies a few minutes later. *I love your new girlfriend. I'm sorry I questioned your judgment earlier.*

She's not my girlfriend, I reply, though when I type the words, it gives me a twinge of something I can't quite put my finger on.

It's not like I want Courtney to be my girlfriend. Dealing with her all the time would be more than I could handle, plus I don't think she could handle *me*, not in my regular CEO life.

Though I still want to go to bed with her. She's passionate. I bet she'd be great in bed.

Okay, I'll admit it. Even though Courtney spends a lot of time trying to push my buttons, I'm enjoying myself. I've missed the companionship of being in a relationship. I always liked that part, but I decided I was finished with relationships after Olivia said she didn't like dating someone who was married to his job and wasn't "emotionally present."

Some men might consider that to be touchy-feely mumbo jumbo, but I didn't. I got what she was saying. It was similar to what many women had told me before. As I didn't see my life-style changing, what was the point in trying to have a girlfriend? Any relationship was doomed.

"When was the last time you went out for gelato or ice cream on a hot summer's day?" Courtney asks.

"Twenty years ago? Maybe more?"

She looks at me like I just kicked a puppy. "But you like it, don't you?"

"Sure. I don't see how you could hate ice cream. I'm not saying I haven't eaten it in twenty years, though I don't think I've had a cone in that long."

"Well, that'll change in ten minutes. I hope we aren't waiting any longer than that."

"Mommy," says Joey the Kid, "you won't make me go twenty years without an ice cream cone, will you? Even if I leave Lego all over the floor and you step on it in the middle of the night?"

～

The gelato is fantastic.

All the seats in the gelateria are full, but we snag a bench in the parkette at the corner. I'm enjoying my lemon cherry sour cream and pistachio, and I'm trying not to look at Courtney because watching her lick her gelato is more than I can bear. The cactus sits between us, a calculated move on my part so I wouldn't be able to shift closer to her without getting poked.

"I can't believe you ordered pistachio," she says. "That's such a boring flavor." Courtney got quince white wine, in addition to the lemon cherry sour cream.

"I hadn't had it in ages, and this one is very good."

"Can I try?"

I hand over my waffle cone, and she takes a nibble of my gelato.

Courtney's mouth. Phallic object. Yeah.

"Why are you looking at me like that?" she asks.

"Like what?"

"Never mind."

"I'm looking at you with fear because I'm afraid you're not going to give that back once you discover the awesomeness of pistachio gelato."

"Did you just saw 'awesomeness'? That's so unlike you."

"You've known me less than twenty-four hours," I point out, though she's correct.

"True." Thankfully, she hands back my gelato cone. "You're right. It's pretty great."

She takes a photo of me with my gelato, and then we eat in silence. When I'm finished, I start to stand up, but she pulls me back down.

"We're going to stay here for a while and people-watch." She points to a man on the other side of the street, hurrying down the sidewalk. "What do you think his story is?"

"He's hurrying because he has a very important meeting."

"Come on. You can do better than that."

"Fine." I can be creative if that's what she wants. "He's divorced and has custody of his five-year-old daughter. He just dropped her off at his ex-wife's for the weekend, then realized he forgot to pack Joey—who is not a phallic cactus, but a cute stuffed koala—in his daughter's overnight bag, and she won't go to sleep without him. He's hurrying home to pick up Joey and bring him to his ex-wife's before his daughter notices Joey isn't there."

Courtney cracks a smile. "That's better." She points at a young couple, maybe in their mid-twenties, who have just walked past the parkette. "What about them?"

Like the man on the other side of the street, they're hurrying, not slowing down to eat gelato and enjoy the sunny day. Normally that would be me, too, and admittedly, it seems rather sad to spend your whole life like that.

"They're rushing home," I say, "because they just said 'I love you' for the first time, and he wants to fuck her brains out."

Courtney's eyes widen.

"Pardon my language. He wants to make sweet, sweet love to her."

I need to stop saying such things around Courtney Kwan.

"Oh?" She looks rather intrigued, or is that just my imagination?

Perhaps she'll change her mind about the casual fling I proposed. I picture her kneeling between my legs, her tongue on my cock, moaning the way she does when she eats ice cream and pineapple buns.

I need another train of thought. I look down and my gaze lands on Joey the Cactus, which doesn't help matters, because Joey really does look like an erect penis. He even has balls.

I choke on my gelato.

"Are you okay?" she asks.

"Something went down funny, that's all."

"I didn't know it was possible to choke on gelato, since it melts in your mouth."

"Uh. There was a whole pistachio. Yes, that's it. A whole pistachio."

Real smooth, Julian.

I swear, I'm normally well-spoken and good at expressing myself, which I can do in several languages, but a part of me feels like an inexperienced teenager when I'm with Courtney. I'm so out of my depth, spending two weeks without work and eating gelato with a woman in the park.

We look at each other for a moment, a moment both awkward and wonderfully full of promise. I pick up the cactus and move it to the other side of me. I'm about to slide my hand onto her knee and see where that leads, but then her phone beeps.

She jumps up, and the moment is ruined.

[10]
COURTNEY

WHEN I LEFT the lab yesterday evening, I wasn't particularly looking forward to my weekend alone, but now I have Julian's company, and I've enjoyed our day together thus far. I've enjoyed being a quirky, silly version of myself—it's easy around him, somehow.

He's been a surprisingly good sport, even as he rolls his eyes and shakes his head when I talk about scrapbooking classes and phallic cacti. I think he's having fun, at least a little, and I'm certainly having fun.

We're sitting in the backyard patio of a coffee shop in Leslieville now. It's lovely here, with cute wooden furniture, trellises with flowers, and purple umbrellas. I dragged him into this place on a whim when I saw the "backyard patio open!" sign, and I'll definitely come back.

I love where I live. It's a short walk from Chinatown East and Greektown on the Danforth, and not too far from Leslieville. There are all sorts of great neighborhoods to explore, all sorts of hidden treasures, like that cactus and succulent shop on Gerrard.

I love Toronto.

And it's nice having Julian with me as I explore the city.

The man is genuinely attracted to me. It's still hard to wrap my head around that, but there have been moments when I swore the air would start sparking from the sexual tension.

Maybe I'm imagining it, but pineapple buns and gelato also taste better in his presence. I wonder what it would be like to lick gelato off his chest.

It's been more than three years since I've had sex, and I miss it. Being skin against skin, holding each other afterward, waking up together. When I'm with Julian, I can't help thinking about it and yearning for it, these things I told myself I'd never have again.

I have to remind myself that there are good reasons for my vow of celibacy, but damn, it's tough when he's sitting across from me, looking so hot in his jeans and polo shirt. He put on the polo shirt before we left, even though there was nothing wrong with the T-shirt he'd been wearing at breakfast. It's like Julian thinks he cannot be seen without a collared shirt in public. But *I* saw him in that T-shirt. He's let me into his private world…sort of. As much as I would allow him.

I have a sip of my pumpkin spice latte. Even though it's only August, this coffee shop has started serving pumpkin spice lattes, or maybe they serve them all year round. It's pretty good, though not quite as good as my regular gingerbread latte at Chris's Coffee Shop.

Julian leans forward. "You don't have to babysit me all day to make sure I don't go into the office or start looking up stock prices. I know you have your own life."

"I don't mind." I lose my train of thought for a moment, slightly distracted by his closeness. "It's not like I have much else to do."

Though it's good to know he doesn't expect me to be with him every hour of the day, because at some point, I'll need some time alone to recharge.

"What do you want to do for dinner?" he asks.

My mind is completely blank, even though I've eaten at dozens and dozens of restaurants in Toronto. I hate when that happens.

I turn the question around. "Where do *you* want to eat? You're the one who's supposed to be having fun, and I've been dragging you around all day."

"Um." His mind seems to have emptied of all rational thought, just like mine, and now he's stroking the back of my hand, which isn't helping my poor brain.

When my brain finally latches onto a word, I blurt it out.

"Tapas!" I say, proud to have come up with something. "I love tapas. I don't care if it's Spanish, I just really like ordering a bunch of small plates and sharing them. It's so much fun."

It's also very date-like.

Just like that fact that he's still stroking my hand.

"Okay," he says, as though my outburst was perfectly normal and did not draw the attention of the women chatting at the table next to ours. "We'll go to Mosaic."

Mosaic is a Middle Eastern small-plates restaurant in Yorkville. It's supposed to be excellent, but I've never been because it's also expensive.

"That's not necessary," I protest, and then I remember who I'm talking to. "Actually, I misspoke. It's totally necessary and we should go there so you can spend your money on me. Although I suspect you need to make a reservation for Saturday dinner a few weeks in advance."

He pulls out his phone. "Let me see what I can do."

An hour later, we're waiting to be shown to a table at Mosaic.

I don't know how Julian did it. I imagine if you're a real celebrity, restaurants would make special accommodations for you, hoping it would bring them attention. But Julian, though rich, isn't a celebrity, and I'm not sure many people would know his name, outside of the Chinese community. And investment bankers, presumably.

"Sorry for keeping you waiting," the hostess says, though we've only been waiting a minute. She flashes Julian a spectacular smile.

I have the urge to wrap my hand around his arm and yell, "Mine!" However, that would be weird, and it might get us kicked out.

And I very much want to eat here.

Plus, he doesn't actually belong to me.

We're led to a table on the rooftop patio. We're not very high up, just on the third floor, so we don't have an impressive view of the city, but it's really nice. There are potted shrubs and flowers and a few well-dressed couples having quiet conversations.

I feel underdressed, but there wasn't time to go back to Julian's to change. We still have Joey the Cactus with us, and Julian places him on the table beside the unlit candle.

"How did you manage this?" I ask as soon as the hostess walks away.

He shrugs. "I know someone. Plus, it's only five fifteen, and I had to promise we'd be done by seven."

I open my menu. Everything sounds so good. I try to ignore the prices—those don't need to factor into my decision.

Of course, money doesn't buy happiness. Well, it probably does if it brings you out of poverty, because living in poverty is stressful and exhausting, but if you have a reasonably comfortable life, like me, money isn't going to buy you happiness. Even though I agreed to this arrangement to get money for the trip and for Naomi, I know this.

Though at the moment, I'm quite happy. I'm practically bouncing in my seat because I'm so excited.

Julian looks at me curiously, and I realize I'm literally bouncing in my seat like a child.

"Were you always like this?" he asks.

I stop bouncing, a little embarrassed. "No. Something happened when I was in undergrad, and for a long time, I couldn't feel joy. At all. When I started to experience joy again, it felt miraculous."

That's the truth without the details.

There are moments when I think my depression is a good thing because it helps me appreciate my mental health when I have it, but mostly, I just wish it away.

Julian looks like he wants to ask me what happened in undergrad, but then he drops his gaze to his menu. "Would you like a bottle of wine?"

"No, that's okay." That's my instinctive response, but then I remember I'm with Julian. "I mean...sure. Yes. We can have wine, but you have to choose because I don't know anything about it."

"Red or white?"

"Whatever you like. I'm not picky."

Our waitress comes around and fills our water glasses. Julian gives her a charming smile. She beams back and he orders something.

"I've never ordered a bottle of wine at a restaurant before," I say after she walks away.

"Really?"

"I've ordered a glass of house wine, but a bottle? No."

When I go out with my family, we don't order alcohol. It's different when it's just me and my sister, but I rarely order more than one drink. With my friends, we're more likely to get a pitcher of sangria.

And dates? Well, I don't date.

The waitress returns with our red wine. She opens the bottle and pours a small amount for Julian. After he tastes it and nods his approval, she pours us each a glass.

I feel so grown-up right now.

He lifts his glass, and I realize he's waiting for me to do the same.

"Cheers," he says, his gaze connecting with mine.

This evening is almost surreal. I'm with Julian Fong on the rooftop patio of a fancy restaurant, sharing a bottle of wine.

I try the wine. "Oh my God. This is practically good enough to give me an orgasm."

He raises his eyebrows, and I clamp my hand over my mouth. I can't believe I said that.

"I mean," I say hurriedly, "it's very good and you have excellent taste. I don't know anything about wine, as I told you before, but I know I like this very much, and please don't ask if I can detect notes of black currants or anything like that."

"I won't," he says, humor in his voice. Then he gives me a heated look, just for a moment, before sipping his wine.

I have to admit, I kind of wish he'd offer to give me an orgasm, even though I'd have to decline.

I finally decide what I want to eat, and we place our order. Our first two dishes arrive fairly quickly. Labneh and lamb ribs. I break off a piece of flatbread and swipe it through the labneh—yogurt cheese—and pop it into my mouth.

Like the wine, it has a nearly orgasmic effect on me, but this time, I choose my words more carefully. "It's delicious."

"I'm glad you like it," Julian says, as though my enjoyment of the food is the most important thing in the world.

The lamb ribs are exquisite, too, and I think they go perfectly with the wine.

It's is the best meal I've ever had.

"Courtney," he says a few minutes later, "you really have to stop making those noises when you eat."

"What noises?"

"You know what I'm talking about." He gives me a look. "The noises that make it sound like someone is pleasuring you."

I don't stop.

~

It's a quarter to seven. We've finished eating and Julian has paid the bill. He refused to let me see it, so I'm not sure how much it cost.

"I'm going to the washroom," he says. "Then we'll head out."

He walks away and I have the last of my wine, but this time, it doesn't taste glorious. This time, I hardly taste anything at all.

I take a deep breath, and when I exhale, there's a heaviness in my chest.

This happens to me every now and then. I call it a "depression attack"—I don't know if there's a technical term for it.

I'll be having a good time and all of a sudden, it feels like I'm moving through molasses and I can't experience anything properly anymore. It'll start happening more often—and last longer— as I approach my once-every-five-years episode of severe depression, and then it'll become all I know.

I don't know what depression is like for other people, but this is what it's like for me.

I take a few more deep breaths, look around, then try to focus on what I can see and hear. Sometimes this stops my thoughts from spiraling, even if I can't fully appreciate my surroundings. Just acknowledging the existence of the outside world is helpful.

I focus on the line of pruned shrubs at the edge of the balcony. The clink of a utensil against a glass. The purple of the tablecloth.

Perhaps it was the alcohol. Usually, alcohol agrees with me just fine, but occasionally, if I have multiple drinks, it has a depressive effect.

The traffic on Cumberland Street below. The smell of lamb and spices…

"Courtney?" Julian says, returning to the table. "Are you ready to go?"

"Yes, I'm just fine," I say, though that wasn't the question he asked.

~

We enter Julian's penthouse. I'm back to feeling normal now, and I'm very much aware of the man standing next to me.

"Thank you," he says. "I had a good time."

"Me, too."

Silence stretches between us.

He looks at his watch. "It's not even seven thirty. We could watch a movie?"

"Sure."

"I have a fancy system." He gestures to the screen on the wall. "But I rarely get to use it."

He decides we should watch *Ocean's Eleven*. He pours himself a scotch, but I decline his offer of a drink—I probably shouldn't drink more alcohol tonight. We sit on his sectional couch, leaving enough space for another person between us, and start the movie.

The gap between us doesn't last long, however. Soon, he pulls me toward him. He doesn't kiss me, just puts his arm around me and holds me close.

I've missed being touched. Not only sexually, but simple touches like this. It's been a decade since a man wrapped his arms around me while we watched a movie together, and it seems like more of a luxury than Julian's expensive home entertainment system. I lean my head on his shoulder and try to pay attention to the screen. Luckily, I've seen this one a few times, so it doesn't require my full attention.

A few minutes later, I hear a noise unrelated to the movie.

Julian is snoring softly.

I smile as I watch this big, important man sleeping like a puppy. Then I extract myself from his embrace, turn off the movie, and bring him a blanket and pillow.

When I get into bed, I imagine his arms around me once more.

I OPEN my eyes and look at my alarm clock.

9:00 am.

That can't be right. I haven't slept this late in years.

I check my phone.

It's definitely nine in the morning.

Last night, Courtney and I had an early dinner, and then we started *Ocean's Eleven*, the 2001 version. Unable to help myself, I pulled Courtney into my arms…and I must have fallen asleep. I only saw about fifteen minutes of the movie. I have a vague recollection of getting up in the middle of the night and moving from the couch to my bed, but other than that, I've been asleep since eight o'clock last night.

Thirteen hours. That's two or three nights' worth of sleep.

I immediately feel guilty. Then I remind myself that I have two weeks off and this is the sort of thing I'm supposed to be doing. I'm supposed to relax and catch up on sleep.

Yesterday was quite successful. I enjoyed wandering around the city with Courtney and seeing the world through her eyes. Appreciating the little things I don't usually have time to appreciate.

I wish she was in my bed now. I want to spend a lazy morning with her, learning every inch of her body. Learning whether she makes the same sounds when she's being touched as she makes when she's eating labneh and drinking good wine, or whether her noises would be even more erotic.

Good God, I can't even imagine.

Somehow, I have to live with her for the next two weeks, a situation entirely of my own making. I don't think I can tolerate two weeks of extreme sexual frustration, especially when she keeps making comments about phallic plants and orgasms in that endearing, slightly awkward way of hers.

Because, fuck, I want to bury myself inside her and coax screams out of her pretty lips, and I have no interest in any other woman, not now.

I still hold out hope that she'll change her mind eventually.

Only so I can take her to bed, though. If I were someone else, perhaps it could be more than a few nights of sex. But unfortunately, that's all I can offer, even if I'm attracted to her more than just physically.

I've tried to have more before, tried it with many different women.

It never works.

I get out of bed and find Courtney in the kitchen, staring at my espresso maker with a bewildered expression. She's wearing shorts and a loose T-shirt, the kind of clothing I imagine she wears around her apartment, and I'm glad she's making herself at home here, even though her presence drives me crazy.

"I'm trying to make a latte," she says, "but I have no idea what I'm doing."

"Let me do it for you."

"No, I want you to teach me, in case you're still asleep when I leave for work tomorrow."

I use this as an excuse to touch her, my hands moving over

hers as I show her what to do, what buttons to press. A few minutes later, she has a latte in a clear glass mug.

"I love your dishes," she says. "Lattes look so pretty in a glass, don't you think?"

"I can't take credit for my dishes. That was Elena."

She wrinkles her nose. It pleases me that she doesn't like thinking of another woman choosing my dishes, but...

"Elena is my housekeeper." I pause. "What do you want to do today?"

"The question is, what do *you* want to do? Don't think of what you *ought* to want to do. Just listen to yourself and tell me the first thing that comes to mind."

The first thing that comes to mind is sex, but I don't tell her that. Instead, I say the second thing, which is totally random.

"Soup dumplings. I want soup dumplings." My mouth starts watering. It's been ages since I've had soup dumplings.

"Should we learn how to make them?"

"No. They're probably fussy to make, and I want them *now*."

She laughs.

I'm already reaching for my phone and clicking on the number of a Chinese dumpling place, which, happily, is open on Sunday mornings.

"What about you?" I ask after I end the call. "What do you want?"

"I hope you ordered enough soup dumplings to share."

"Well..." I pretend to ponder this for a while. "Maybe."

"Julian!" She hits me playfully on the shoulder. "Order me some dim sum, then. Be sure to get *cheong fan*."

I make another phone call.

"Wow," she says. "You really think we can eat all that?"

"I'm hungry." Even though I haven't worked out yet today, apparently thirteen hours of sleep is good for one's appetite. Now that I think of it, it's been ages since I've been truly ravenous like this. My appetite hasn't been the greatest lately.

Courtney looks at me over her latte. "How many languages do you speak?"

Right. She heard me speak English, Cantonese, and Mandarin in the last three minutes.

"I speak five fluently. French and Toisanese, in addition to what you already heard."

"What did you speak at home?"

"English, usually. Both my parents were born here. Some Toisanese, but that was mostly with my grandparents."

My brothers don't speak any Chinese languages fluently, although they know a little, but languages were always easy for me.

"What about other languages?" she asks. "You said you speak five *fluently*."

"Spanish, Japanese, and German."

She looks at me, wide-eyed. "You make me feel like a failure. I speak Cantonese, but my French is shit and my Mandarin is even worse."

"You have a PhD. Not many people go that far in school. *I* don't have a PhD."

"Maybe not, Mr. Moneybags, but I'm sure you're smart enough to get one if that's what you wanted. But, no, you're too busy running the world."

The last thing I want is to make her feel inferior. "You are—"

"Forget I said that." She waves her hand away from her. "It's all good. I'm happy with my life." A shadow briefly passes over her face, but I know she won't tell me what it's about, even though I want to know all about her.

Forty-five minutes later, I set out plates and chopsticks, and Courtney opens up all the food that was delivered.

"This smells amazing," she says.

It tastes amazing, too. Even the *cheong fan* is good, though rice noodle rolls aren't my favorite. But the soup dumplings are certainly the best.

Or maybe the best part is that Courtney is sitting across from me.

~

We're reading in lounge chairs on my rooftop patio. About two-thirds of the rooftop is available for anyone in the building to enjoy, but the rest of it is mine, although I rarely come up here. Courtney was aghast when she learned this and insisted we make good use of it. Since I'd finished *Como agua para chocolate*, she dragged me to the bookstore and ordered me to pick out a book without first doing research and reading reviews. An attempt to make me more spontaneous, I guess. I had to choose a book based only on the cover and blurb—the horror!

The thriller I selected is pretty good so far, although I've only read six pages because I keep looking at Courtney. She's sitting across from me, her legs stretched out and crossed at the ankles. She's wearing a pink sundress that goes down to her knees, and if she uncrossed her legs…

I can't stop thinking about it.

Anyway, I'm supposed to be reading, not ogling her.

We read in silence for an hour, and it's comfortable just being with her like this. Together, but not feeling the need to entertain each other. I'd be able to read twice as fast if she weren't here, but I wouldn't wish it any other way. I feel a sense of peace when I'm with her, even if I want to lick every inch of her body. Unlike usual, I don't feel the need to push myself and be as efficient as possible. It's rather nice.

She glances up and catches me looking at her, and I don't hide what I've been doing.

I smile at her lazily. "I'm enjoying the view."

She rolls her eyes.

"What?" I say. "It's true."

"You're such a charmer."

"Not really. That's Vince."

She tilts her head to the side. "No, I think it's you." Then she mutters, under her breath, "At least that's what you do to *me*." She returns her attention to her book, but I'm not ready to let it go, not quite yet.

I put down my novel. "Is that so? Tell me more about what I do to you. I'm curious."

"I think you're fully aware of your effect on women. You're smart, rich, and good-looking, and you have an intensity that's irresistible."

"You seem to be doing a pretty good job of resisting. And I don't care about my effect on other women, only on *you*."

"You can be very good at flattery when you want to be."

I slide to the edge of my chair. I pick up one of her feet and start to massage it.

She moans. "That feels so good."

I keep going. I want to spoil her. "Would you like a pedicure? I can arrange that."

"Are you offering to give me one yourself?"

"No, I'm offering to throw my money around again."

"How about this. I'll get a mani-pedi if you get one, too. We can go together." She grins. "Some men do them, you know. You don't have to have your nails painted red—you can skip that part. Yes! We should definitely do this."

Courtney is dangerous. She has me seriously considering a pedicure. Vince would laugh his head off.

"I'll think about it," I say, putting down her foot and picking up the other. She groans as I press my thumb into her arch.

"I'll take that as a yes."

"I said I'd think about it."

"Good enough for me," she says.

I glare at her, and she laughs.

This woman will be the death of me.

∼

Courtney holds the wooden spoon up to my lips.

"No," I say. "I'll eat my cookies once they've been in the oven, thank you very much."

We're baking chocolate chip cookies. Her idea, not mine. I can cook a little but I've never baked before. I'm kind of grossed out by all the butter we put in the dough, though that's not the issue right now.

"There's raw egg in the cookie dough."

"Live dangerously for once," she says.

"Salmonella is very unpleasant."

"I'm aware of the existence of salmonella, but it's rare, and kids have been eating chocolate chip cookie dough for generations. I bet nothing bad will happen. I did this many times when I was little."

"Your mother baked a lot?

"Sometimes."

"Mine never did." I examine the spoon. "I don't think this is a good idea."

She puts her hand on her hip. "If you had a compromised immune system, I'd agree, but you're young and healthy, aren't you?"

I nod. "I'm still not doing this."

"Suit yourself." She brings the spoon to her own lips.

I don't want to eat cookie dough, but that doesn't mean I want her to eat it instead.

I yank the spoon away from Courtney as images of her getting a foodborne illness flash through my mind. Before she can stop me, I've licked every last bit of dough off the wooden spoon.

"Good, isn't it?" she asks.

"Yes," I admit, "it is."

"You got the spoon, so I'll take the bowl." She swipes her

finger through dough clinging to the edge of the ceramic bowl, but I wrap my hand around her wrist before she can bring it to her mouth.

I do it because I'm afraid of her getting ill. And because the cookie dough really is good and I want more.

But mostly, I do it because I want her finger in my mouth.

I swirl my tongue over her finger then suck on it.

She gasps.

"Not fair," she says. It comes out as a whisper. "That was my cookie dough."

"Fine. You can have some, too, since you're so insistent."

I swipe up the last of the dough, including a chocolate chip, on my finger and hold it to her lips. She sucks on my finger, which makes me think all sorts of delicious thoughts. When I pull back my hand, I'm breathing hard.

I can't stop myself from dipping my head, but I pause when my lips are a finger's breadth from hers. She nods, and I take her mouth in mine.

The kiss tastes like chocolate chip cookies and butter and *her*...and that's the best part, finally being able to taste her after a weekend in her presence.

"Julian," she groans.

She's said my name many times before, but never like this.

I fit my hands under her ass and pick her up. She clings to me as I walk to the couch and sit down, kissing her the whole time. I slide my lips to the underside of her jaw and plant open-mouthed kisses there. Her lips are parted in pleasure and her eyes are shut. Oh, God.

Her hands slip under my shirt and up my chest; she murmurs in appreciation.

"Yes," I whisper, cupping her cheeks then sliding my fingers into her hair, which I've been longing to touch for ages. I tip her mouth to mine again and slant my lips over hers, taking and giving all that I can, trying to get closer and closer, overjoyed that

I finally have this woman in my arms. She's a passionate kisser, as I knew she would be.

Ding! Ding!

What the fuck is that? Whatever it is, it won't make me stop kissing Courtney.

I press her against me, her breasts squeezed between us, and oh, those should definitely be bare right now.

I'm bunching up the bottom of her shirt when I hear that blasted sound again.

Ding! Ding!

"It's the oven timer." She sounds a bit dazed. "We need to take the cookies out."

Dammit, why did we decide to make cookies?

But I shouldn't complain because the cookie dough led to our kiss.

Courtney jumps up. She takes the pans out of the oven and lets the cookies cool for a couple minutes before using a spatula to put them on the wire rack.

"We'll let them cool a little longer," she says, wiping her hands. "Then we can eat them. The danger of baking is that you're tempted to eat too many at once, but—"

"Courtney," I interrupt. "I want you in my bed tonight."

JULIAN KISSED ME SENSELESS, so senseless that I'm considering going to his bed right this minute. That's the only thing I crave right now—not the chocolate chip cookies cooling on the rack, but him. Although I've felt sexually frustrated in the past few years, I haven't *craved* being with a man until now.

But Julian is special.

And if I go to bed with him, it will get even worse.

If I weren't approaching the five-year mark, if I weren't convinced my descent into depression would begin any day, maybe I'd risk it. However, now is not the time to be taking risks.

And yet, I'm living with him.

I should walk away from this situation right now, but I want the money he promised me, and I don't want to miss out on spending two weeks with him, dangerous as it is.

I draw the line at going to bed with him, though.

"I'm sorry," I whisper. "I can't."

He tilts his head to the side. "You're a hedonist, except for this."

"I wouldn't call myself a hedonist."

He breaks off a small piece of a warm chocolate chip cookie. He holds it up to my lips, and I eat the cookie from his hand.

I moan in bliss.

He swallows hard. I'm thankful he isn't kissing me again, but on the other hand, I'm devastated he isn't kissing me again.

I put two cookies on a plate. "I need some time alone. I'll be in the guest room."

I can feel his eyes on me as I walk down the hall.

It's Monday morning, and I'm glad I have to work today. It'll be good to have some time apart from Julian after what happened yesterday.

Right now, we're eating breakfast together like a married couple, but soon I'll be on my way. Julian has already worked out and showered, his hair slightly wet.

I want to touch it, but I don't.

He has a gym in his penthouse, and I peeked inside while he was lifting weights. Not gonna lie, it was pretty hot, his muscles rippling under his T-shirt. He saw me standing at the door and winked at me, and I nearly asked if he'd consider working out shirtless, but thankfully, I managed to keep my mouth shut.

Now I'm eating Cheerios, and he's eating some kind of freaky high-protein cereal.

"Is that stuff any good?" I ask.

He slides his bowl toward me. "Try it."

I take a bite and grimace. "It tastes like hamster food."

"Does it?"

I nod. "It does."

"How do you know what hamster food tastes like?"

Oh, this is embarrassing.

"We had a pet hamster when I was a kid. I thought the food

pellets looked tasty and figured if the hamster could eat it, why couldn't I?"

He doubles over in laughter. I'm glad the story made him laugh, and I can't help joining in.

"Julian?" says an unfamiliar female voice.

I immediately sit up straight and force myself to stop laughing. Why the hell is there another woman in his condo?

I turn to see an older white woman, and I breathe out a sigh of relief. This must be his housekeeper.

"I'm sorry," she says. "I wouldn't have let myself in if I'd known you had company."

"Don't worry, it's fine," he says. "Courtney is heading off to work in a few minutes. Courtney, this is Elena, my housekeeper."

"It's not what you're thinking," I say. "We're just friends."

I think of that kiss.

Right. Just friends.

Keep telling yourself that, Courtney.

Elena rolls her eyes. "I wasn't born yesterday. If Julian has a guest at eight o'clock in the morning, she's not just a friend."

I'm not sure how to respond.

"Courtney's working for me," Julian says. "I went into the office on Friday because I didn't know what to do with myself. I need to figure out how to have fun, and she's helping me with that."

"Uh-huh," Elena says. "If that's what you kids call it these days."

She heads to another part of the penthouse, and a moment later, I hear the vacuum cleaner. I assume she's trying to give us some privacy.

I push Julian's bowl of hamster food back toward him and have one last bite of Cheerios.

"I take my second career as a how-to-enjoy-life coach very seriously," I say. "I will be checking up on you throughout the day, and you better not be in the middle of putting on a suit to head to a meeting, okay?"

"Yes, ma'am," he says, suppressing a smile.

I stand up. It's time for me to leave, but it doesn't feel right to leave, not like this. There's something missing.

I bend over and kiss him on the lips. I intend for it to be a quick peck, but once I feel the sweet pressure of his lips against mine, I need more. I open for him, and he takes that as an invitation. One of his arms slides around my back, his hand slipping through my hair, and I moan against him.

I miss kissing.

It's only a kiss—what can it hurt? I showed incredible restraint by not walking into the gym earlier, removing his sweaty T-shirt, and dropping to my knees. I deserve a reward.

"Have a good day," I say, pulling back.

"You, too," he murmurs.

I'll be thinking about him all day.

My phone beeps at ten in the morning, and I smile when I see it's a text from Courtney.

What are you up to? she asks.

Baking lemon squares so I have something to feed my family when they come over, I reply.

Your family's visiting today? You didn't tell me.

They didn't say anything, but I know they're coming.

There's a zero percent chance I won't get a surprise visit from either Vince or my mother today, if not my entire family. I suppose it's not really a surprise if I know it's coming, but I don't know when it'll happen, and I intend to be ready. As soon as Courtney left for work, I looked up a bunch of recipes online then headed to the grocery store to buy ingredients.

By lunchtime, I've made lemon squares and lemon rosemary shortbread. When Courtney texts to check up on me again, I send her a picture of the baked goods.

Marry me, she says.

I stare at the text message, wondering how to reply.

I'm kidding, she adds a moment later. *I can't believe you baked all that when you've only baked once before in your life. How are you so good at everything?*

Save the compliments until you've tried them. Want me to bring a lemon square to the lab now?

You already packed two chocolate chip cookies in my lunch. I think that's enough.

Yes, I did pack her lunch this morning. A sandwich and carrot sticks and the cookies we made yesterday.

I'm becoming quite domestic, much to Elena's amusement.

I really do want to visit Courtney at work, though. First of all, because I'm running out of ideas for how to entertain myself. And second of all, because I desperately want another kiss.

I was pleasantly surprised when she kissed me goodbye this morning, and although it was only a brief kiss, it was hardly chaste, and I've been replaying it in my mind all morning. Normally, I'd be able to wrestle control of my thoughts, but I can't seem to do that today. I have no work to occupy me, and Courtney Kwan captivates me like no one else.

At two o'clock, I'm reading on my rooftop patio, a couple of lemon squares—I really did a great job with those, if I do say so myself—and a beer on the table beside me.

"Hey."

I jump at Elena's voice.

"If you don't need anything else, I'm heading out now," she says.

"Sure."

"And your brother's here."

Of course he is.

I sit up and look into Vince's smirking face.

"I never thought I'd see the day," he says. "You, reading and drinking a beer in the middle of the afternoon. Enjoying the sunshine."

"It's only one beer," I say, suddenly defensive, "and I'm under the umbrella and I still put on sunscreen, so I'm not going to get burnt."

"Glad to hear you haven't really changed." He picks up my beer. "Labatt 50? Seriously?"

"What's wrong with Labatt 50?"

"It's an old man beer, but I guess that's appropriate, seeing as you usually have about as much fun as an old man."

"Thanks for the compliment."

He shoves his hands in his pockets and rocks back on his heels. "I just came to give you a heads-up. Mom and Po Po should be here any minute."

"You told them, didn't you?"

"Told them what? That you have a new girlfriend and she's living with you? Why, yes, I did. I like Courtney, by the way. She sent me all sorts of pictures from your fun weekend together—I particularly enjoyed the picture of Joey the Phallic Cactus. I can't wait to see the results of your private scrapbooking lessons. And apparently you're getting a pedicure?"

"I did not agree to that. I told her I'd think about it. Why are you and Courtney suddenly best buddies? And how are you texting her now that I have my phone back?"

"She sent me her number before she returned your phone." Vince studies me for a moment. "You're still too tense."

"Maybe that has something to do with your presence."

He ignores my comment. "You're not getting laid yet, are you? If you're determined to keep things platonic with Courtney, at least let me—"

"Stop trying to arrange orgies for me!"

"Yeah, you definitely need to get laid."

"I want to," I mutter, "but she's not interested."

Well, she's clearly attracted to me, and she makes pretty damn erotic noises when she kisses me, plus I can't imagine she'd have anything against having sex just for fun. But she says she can't, and she won't tell me why.

Vince finds this hilarious. "You need serious help with women."

"May I remind you that I'm the one who's had several relationships in the past ten years, whereas you haven't had a girlfriend since Deanna?"

"I…" He shakes his head.

My brother, at a loss for words. Huh.

As I'm pondering this unusual situation, I hear some banging noises in my condo, so I head downstairs with my book and half-finished beer.

Mom and Po Po are here.

"Julian!" Mom says. "There you are."

I pull out the containers of cookies and lemon squares. I arrange them on a platter and start the kettle for tea.

Vince is back to his usual smirking self. "Wow. Courtney wasn't lying when she said you'd been baking."

"You made these?" Mom asks. "Not Elena?"

"I did."

Po Po grabs a lemon square and takes a bite. "Pretty good. Your girlfriend helped you?"

"Just with the chocolate chip cookies. I made the rest myself." Then I register her words. "Courtney isn't my girlfriend."

"She's living with you, yes? Sounds like a girlfriend to me."

I don't know why I'm arguing when there's no chance of me convincing my family that I do not have a girlfriend, not after Vince put that idea in their heads.

The water boils. I make a pot of jasmine tea and bring it to the dining room table, along with the platter of cookies and squares. I return to the kitchen for my bottle of beer.

"This is your fourth day off work," Mom says, "and you've already gotten a girlfriend and learned to bake?"

"He's efficient even in his time off," Vince says.

Po Po taps my bottle of beer. "Do not approve of this." She clucks her tongue. "If you're not careful, you will turn into Vince."

"Hey!" he says. "What's wrong with me?"

I'm about to answer, but then my grandmother lifts the beer to her lips. We all watch, wide-eyed, as she chugs the rest of the bottle.

"There," she says proudly. "Now you can't drink it."

"There are twenty-three more bottles in the fridge," I say.

"You bought a two-four of Labatt 50?" Vince laughs. "God, you are such an old man. And Po Po, that was impressive. But why is it okay for you to drink beer in the middle of the afternoon, and not for us?"

"Am eighty-nine." She points to herself. "Could drop dead any minute. Doesn't matter what I do anymore."

"Ma," my mother says, "will you please stop talking about dropping dead?"

"Why? It's true. But it would be nice to have great-grandchildren first."

"I'm sorry to tell you this," I say, "but there's a good chance you won't get any great-grandchildren, unless Vince forgets to use protection when he's high on drugs."

My brother discreetly gives me the middle finger.

"I'm not counting on Vince," she says, "but *you*. You have nice girlfriend now, yes? Vince says she's nice. Chinese girl with PhD. Sounds like good match."

I sigh. "She's not my girlfriend."

"Just to be clear," Mom says, "we don't care if she's Chinese. It's not important, as long as you love her."

"I care," Po Po says. "Just a little."

"You're old-fashioned."

"Am eighty-nine and could drop dead any minute! Am allowed to be old-fashioned." Po Po turns to me. "If you have girlfriend who is not Chinese, it's okay. Still happy for you. But I think it's better this way. Where is she?" Po Po looks around.

"Unlike me," I say, "Courtney isn't taking two weeks off work. She's at the lab."

"Where does she work?" Mom asks.

"At U of T."

"Will she quit when you marry?" Po Po asks. "Stay home to take care of babies?"

Dammit. Drinking beer and eating lemon squares alone on the patio was a much better way of spending the afternoon than facing an inquisition about the girlfriend I do not have.

"There won't be any babies, not if Julian can't seal the deal," Vince says.

"Seal the deal?" Po Po frowns. "What does this mean?"

My family insisted I take time off so I wouldn't burn out, but now they're insisting on driving me up the wall.

"Stop it. All of you. For the last time, Courtney is not my girlfriend. Even if she were, I just met her on Friday, and it would be way too soon to start talking about marriage and babies, okay? Why can't you all leave me alone to drink my old man beer in peace?"

There's a moment of silence.

And then my phone beeps.

Vince swipes it off the table and reads the message. "Courtney wants to make sure you haven't cracked and gone into work."

"I've definitely cracked," I mutter.

He scrolls through our message history. "Ooh, listen to this! She asked him to marry her."

"She did not—I mean, that was a joke."

Vince shrugs. "Details, details."

I grab my phone back before any more damage can be done.

"I want to meet her," Po Po says. "Not leaving until she gets here."

Mom nods in agreement. "I'm very curious."

"Hey, I've got nothing else to do," Vince says, reaching for a cookie. "I'll stay, too, even though I've already met her."

Since I don't see any way out of this, I text Courtney and ask if she can leave work early.

~

Courtney arrives before four o'clock, which is incredible. I've never gotten home from work anywhere close to four o'clock.

"I'm sorry," I murmur as I meet her at the door.

"That's okay," she says, slipping off her shoes. "Hey, Vince."

He comes over and they give each other a hug. I can't say I'm too fond of that.

"How's Joey the Phallic Cactus?" he asks. "I hear he's staying in your room."

Po Po struggles to her feet. "I know what a cactus is, but what is phallic cactus?"

"Forget about it, Ma," Mom mutters. "It's not important."

Mom and Po Po come to the door.

"This is Courtney," I tell them. "She's not my girlfriend, but you wanted to meet her, so here she is. Courtney, these are my mother and grandmother."

Po Po beams. "Very pretty. You make cute babies."

I'd hoped we'd be able to go five minutes without the mention of babies, but apparently that was too much to ask.

Courtney laughs uncomfortably. "Julian and I are just friends."

"See?" I say. "She confirmed it. Just friends."

Friends who have shared a couple kisses.

"Aiyah." Po Po shakes her head and turns to Courtney. "Why not? Julian is very handsome and rich. Good catch."

"I know. He's a very good catch." Courtney's gaze is on me, and heat prickles my skin.

Po Po puts her hand on Courtney's arm, and I'll grudgingly

admit it's nice that my family has taken to Courtney, but at this point, they'd be thrilled with practically any woman.

But she's different.

"You work hard, too?" Po Po asks Courtney. "Like Julian? All focused on career?"

"Something like that," Courtney mumbles.

Vince swaggers over and slaps me on the back. "No, she's the fun one. She's living with him so she can teach him how to have a good time on his vacation."

"I'm so confused," Mom says. "You're not actually dating? You're just friends, but you're living together?"

Courtney nods. "Temporarily."

"Vince's explanation is correct," I say. "For once."

My brother gives me a dirty look.

"But you like each other," Mom says, frowning.

"As friends," Courtney clarifies, but she smiles at me and tucks a lock of hair behind her ear.

"You should kiss!" Po Po says. "Maybe if you kiss, everything will change! Have seen this in movies."

"Go on." Vince nudges me toward Courtney. "Kiss each other in front of your family. It'll be just like you're getting married."

Courtney looks stricken. She must find my family overwhelming.

I don't blame her.

"Ah." Po Po nods sagely. "You prefer to do this in private. I get the hint." She clutches my mother's arm. "Come on. You, too, Vince. We're leaving. Though, maybe…maybe I'll take one more lemon square first."

I grab a lemon square for my grandmother, grateful she's going to drag my mother and brother out of here. I was afraid they'd be here for hours, interrogating Courtney.

"Fine, fine," Vince grumbles. "I'll stop pissing you off and get on with my exciting life."

"I'm sure you will," I say.

Still, it takes another ten minutes to get my family into the elevator. When they're finally gone, I walk over to Courtney and wrap my arms around her. She doesn't embrace me back, but she doesn't step away from me, either.

We stand like this for a few minutes. She stares out the south-facing window that she admired so much the first time she saw it, but today, her eyes look vacant.

"You okay?" I ask, pulling her closer. "I'm sorry about my family. They mean well, but they can be a bit much. I was half-afraid my grandmother would go to my bedroom and look through my closet to see if you'd moved your stuff in."

"Your family clearly loves you very much," she says. "Where was your father?"

"At the office, helping out in my absence." I hesitate, not sure if I should ask the question I want to ask. I try to keep it light. "What are your parents like? Would they be thrilled if you brought someone home?"

"They'd be thrilled if I brought *you* home. My mom would brag about it to all her friends." She laughs a little. "My parents don't tease me anymore. I know it probably seems bothersome to you, but I miss it. It's like they don't know how to act around me. Not since…"

I know she's talking about whatever happened in undergrad. I want her to tell me, but I also know she's not going to, not now. That's okay.

I pull her to the couch and into my lap. We kiss lazily for a few minutes.

When we come up for air, she's smiling, and nothing could make me happier.

IT WAS Vince's mention of marriage. I wasn't prepared for that, and I was suddenly filled with longing. To have a husband and in-laws like the Fongs. Not because of their wealth, but because they genuinely seem like good people, and they were excited to meet me. I also enjoyed seeing them tease Julian.

It was a longing for something I can never have.

But in the twenty-four hours since then, I've mostly managed to push that out of my mind, and last night, there was some pretty hot and heavy kissing before bed. I was lying underneath Julian on the couch, and he was kissing me *everywhere*. I didn't want him to remove any of my clothes, and he seemed to understand that without me telling him. But his cock was hard and heavy between us and, God, it was tempting.

Today at the lab, I could hardly think of anything but being naked in bed with him.

It's only Tuesday. We still have twelve more days together.

I don't know how I'm going to survive this, but I'm determined to do it and get my five thousand dollars, which is why I head to Chris's Coffee Shop after work to meet my sister.

"Hey." Naomi sits down across from me, coffee in hand. She looks at me for a moment, then says, "You haven't slept with him yet. That's the problem, isn't it?"

"Yes," I groan. "Last night, after I met his family—"

"You met his family? What's his dad like? I'm curious."

"His father wasn't there. Anyway, after that, Julian and I made dinner together, then we played Scrabble—"

"Which you won, naturally, since you always win at Scrabble."

"No, he won. Because Julian is a freak of nature and he's amazing at everything."

Her mouth falls open. "You lost a game of Scrabble? For real?"

"Quit distracting me. Anyway, then we watched a movie." *Ocean's Eleven*—he managed to stay awake this time. "Afterward, there was some, um, kissing. A lot of kissing. And this wasn't the first time."

"Hmm. You say he's amazing at everything, so it's only natural to conclude—"

"Believe me, I think about it constantly." I have a sip of my gingerbread latte, but that doesn't hide the heat rushing to my cheeks.

"I know you have trouble separating sex from the other stuff, but it *is* possible. I've done it many times. You don't have to develop feelings for every guy you sleep with."

"You're different from me. Plus, the last time you insisted it was 'just sex,' you ended up falling for the guy."

"Yep, and now we're together and it's awesome. That could happen to you, too."

I realize my mistake in talking to Naomi about this. She's happily in love and that's all she can see.

But my sister is my best friend. She's the only one who always stuck by me. When I first had problems with depression in high school, my parents were in denial despite what the doctor told them. My mother eventually came around and understood that I really was sick, but now she just walks on eggshells and tries not to upset me.

My father is still in denial and thinks I'm just weak.

Dad and I don't talk much anymore. I used to be my father's girl, and when I was little, he would help me with my science kits and always encouraged my interests. He supported my desire to be a scientist and didn't push me to be a doctor, unlike some of my friends' parents. But after that episode when I was sixteen, nothing was quite the same. When I went on leave from university and moved back home, we mostly spoke through my mother.

"If you were actually sick," he said, "the medications would work."

Yet, no matter how many drugs I tried, nothing changed except the side effects.

Many years ago, my aunt told me that their father—my paternal grandfather—had killed himself back in Hong Kong. I was shocked. I knew he'd died before I was born, but I'd never known much about him. Sometimes I wonder if my father's denial is because he fears I will end my life like his own father and can't bear to think of it, but I'm not sure.

My friends didn't stick by me, either. Not in high school, not in university, and that hurt. After I finally finished undergrad—a year late—and started grad school, I kept my issues to myself. When I didn't feel good, I'd pretend everything was fine. I became good at faking it.

Naomi was always there, though, and I always told her the truth.

"Look," she says, taking my hand, "if you get depressed again—"

"I'm not sure why you don't think it's inevitable. Once you've had three episodes of depression like I have, the chances of it happening again are very, very high."

"Okay, *when* it happens again, I bet it'll be better than last time."

"Why do you say that?"

"Well, last time was better than the time before, wasn't it?"

"It was still really fucking bad," I say.

"You're in Toronto with me now, rather than in Kingston. You know yourself better. You've been more stable in the past few years."

Even though my episodes of severe depression happen once every five years, that doesn't mean I'm completely healthy in between. I feel like my mental health is in a precarious position, like it's something I'll always have to treat with care. But it's true that I've been reasonably healthy since I started my job at U of T two years ago. I'm better at taking care of myself now and have coping strategies I didn't have before. Whenever I make a decision, I ask myself, "Is this good for my mental health?" When I'm in a particularly bad spot and struggle with suicidal thoughts, the question is closer to, "Will this kill me?" but the idea is the same.

The reason for my self-imposed ban on sex is because of my mental health. I get attached easily and cannot afford a repeat of what happened with Dane, yet another person who didn't stick by me.

"I know you're thinking about Dane," Naomi says, "but the reason that hurt so much was because you'd been together for a year and a half, and he ditched you at the worst point in your life. Anyway, I'm not saying you should definitely sleep with Julian, but maybe let yourself have fun and see where it goes. You could end up like me and Will."

"Julian's already told me he doesn't do relationships."

"What are his reasons for that?"

"He works too hard. He doesn't have time for a girlfriend." I blow out a breath. "It's definitely tempting to go to bed with him, though. Just a little fun. I'm not sure it's realistic to deny myself sex for the rest of my life."

When I came up with my no-sex-for-Courtney plan more than three years ago, it was after a few sexual encounters—satisfying, but not mind-blowing—with a grad student in the history department. I started getting attached and he didn't. I figured sex wasn't worth the hassle. I could satisfy my own needs, couldn't I?

For the past three years, that's been enough for me.

But when I feel Julian on top of me, kissing his way down my neck, I know no toy could do what he's capable of. The no-sex-for-Courtney rule no longer seems reasonable.

I miss sex. I miss physical intimacy. And Julian is right there, very willing.

"Well, *I* couldn't give up sex," Naomi says. "But I'm not you. I understand why this is difficult for you."

"Sex releases endorphins," I say, thinking out loud. "Endorphins are good for you. They make you happy."

This might be good for my mental health after all. Sure, there could be a few of those pesky feelings involved, but I suddenly feel like I can handle them. Besides, I won't have too much time with him—less than two weeks. How attached could I get in two weeks? It's nothing like Dane.

Naomi chuckles. "Sounds like you've talked yourself into it."

I nod, happy with my decision. "I'm going to create some endorphins tonight."

~

After finishing my gingerbread latte, I head home, and by "home," I mean Julian's penthouse. Weird how I've started thinking of it as home.

Julian isn't in the living room or on the rooftop patio, and if he was going out, he would have told me. I check his bedroom. It's the first time I've seen his bedroom, actually. His bed is enormous, and my heart rate speeds up as I imagine us rolling around in it together.

But he's not in his bedroom, not now.

I glance at the doors leading to his washroom and closet, and it gives me an idea. I head to his closet, which is full of fancy business clothes, and select a pale blue dress shirt. I hang it up in my room before continuing my search for Julian.

I find him in his home office, reading a report.

"What the hell is this?" I ask, as though I've caught him doing something truly awful.

He looks at me sheepishly. "I ran out of things to do."

I pull the report out of his hand and sit on his lap. "Do you want me to call your parents? Tell them you're working on your week off? Or should I call Vince and ask him to drag you to a crack-filled sex dungeon?"

He chuckles as he wraps his arms around me, and then his lips are on mine.

"Mm," he says. "I think *you* should punish me instead."

"What should I do?"

"You're the one doing the punishing. It's your choice."

I take his mouth again and slide my tongue against his. He moans low in his throat. It's amazing, this power I have with him. I slip my hand under his polo shirt and scrape my nails over his abs, which elicits another moan.

"Courtney," he murmurs.

I squirm on his lap as I kiss him, and his erection presses between my legs. I don't need to hold myself back. I can take him inside me tonight and feel what I haven't felt in years.

The thought freaks me out.

I'd totally planned to do this today, but I've only had sex a handful of times in the past ten years, and although Julian isn't a partying womanizer like his brother, I'm sure there's no shortage of women who want to sleep with him. Doubtless he's had lots of sex with lots of beautiful women who know how to please a man. I'm not jealous, not exactly; I'm just suddenly very self-conscious.

I know he wants me, yet I'm afraid I'll disappoint him. Not so much because I'm hardly a model underneath my clothes, but because I'm not very experienced.

I break the kiss and lean back. "Let's go out, away from the temptation of work."

"To my office at Fong Investments?" Julian asks.

I laugh.

"It's very private and soundproof." He raises his eyebrows. "Just saying."

I push him playfully as I get to my feet. "No, we're going drinking."

After a couple cocktails and a steak dinner—my God, I'm going to gain so much weight—we return home and head to our separate bedrooms. I take off my clothes, except for my underwear, and put on the shirt I stole from his closet earlier. I don't have any nice lingerie, but there's something sexy about a woman wearing a man's dress shirt, isn't there? The sleeves are long, and the bottom of the shirt falls midway down my thighs, but the shirt isn't huge on me otherwise—I'm not a slender woman. That's okay. I still look sexy, right? I can strut into his room and climb into his bed and…

I pull off the shirt.

No, I can't do this.

Wednesday at work, I'm practically useless. I can't stop thinking about what would have happened if I hadn't lost my nerve, if I'd gone to Julian's bedroom last night.

You would have disappointed him, says a little voice in my head.

Fuck that little voice. We would have had spectacular sex, and he wouldn't have been able to keep his hands off me.

Yes, I'm a bit scared, but I can't keep listening to that fear.

I'm going to create some endorphins, and nobody's going to stop me.

After work, Julian and I walk by the lake and wander through the Music Garden. Then he makes me lamb chops for dinner before we binge-watch *Stranger Things*. I'm horrified that he's never seen it and that he's never watched more than two episodes of a show in a row. We say goodnight to each other after three episodes, but in my head, it's *goodnight for now*.

I go to my room and undress. With shaking hands, I put on his blue shirt again and button it up. Then I tiptoe to his bedroom, as though I'm doing something illicit and don't want to be caught. But there's absolutely nothing wrong with taking some pleasure for myself.

I deserve it.

My heart beats quickly as I approach Julian's bedroom. I knock on the door, then immediately open it and let myself in.

"Hey," I say, standing just inside the door.

He's reading in bed, head propped up on a few pillows, and he's wearing boxers and a plain white T-shirt. He's gorgeous.

He looks me up and down. "You're not wearing pants."

"I'm not wearing pants."

"And you're wearing my shirt."

"I thought it would look—"

"Sexy." He pauses. "It's very sexy."

My heart is still hammering, a combination of excitement and fear.

He puts his novel on the bedside table, his gaze never leaving me. The air between us practically crackles.

"Come here." He pats the mattress.

I go and sit on the edge of the bed.

"You told me you couldn't do this," he says.

"I changed my mind. I want that fling. But I have to tell you something." I swallow and fiddle with the collar of the shirt. "I haven't had sex in three years. Actually, I've had very little sex in the past ten years. So, if it seems like I don't know what I'm doing, it's because I'm horribly out of practice."

"Shh." He presses a finger to my lips. "Don't worry about that. I'll take good care of you tonight." He rolls me onto my back, and I melt into the pillows. "Let me take care of you."

"Thank you," I whisper.

JULIAN BEGINS TO UNDRESS ME. He takes his time with the buttons on the shirt, as though each one must be undone just so. Once he's slid the last button through the hole, he parts the sides of the shirt and looks at me reverently. Then he bends down and kisses my nipples as though they're in need of worshipping.

"If you don't like something, tell me," he says. "Or if you really like something, feel free to tell me that, too."

We're supposed to be having a fling. In my mind, a fling conjures up images of a rough fuck against the door or over the desk—we could have done that if I'd made a move when we were in his home office yesterday.

But I have to learn about sex all over again, and I don't think I could manage dirty and rough, not yet.

I also think I can count on him to give me exactly what I need.

He lifts up my back so he can remove the shirt, then lays me back down on the bed. I am naked now, except for my underwear, and he smiles as his gaze slides over my body. He runs his finger up my leg to my thigh and touches my wetness through my panties.

"I'll take care of that for you tonight," he murmurs.

He sits up and shucks off his shirt, followed by his boxers.

No woman would be disappointed with the way Julian looks when he's naked. He's solid and muscled with a light dusting of dark hair on his chest. Although I had a pretty good idea of what he would look like without clothes—I'd spent an awful lot of time thinking about it, in fact—it's not the same as the real thing.

He smiles when he sees me checking him out, my gaze lingering on his cock. I'm a little self-conscious about being almost naked, but he isn't, not at all.

He crawls on top of me and drops his forehead to mine as he slips his hand inside my underwear. He runs his hand over my slit, which is enough to make me gasp. Gently, he pushes the tip of his finger inside me, and I gasp again.

"Okay?" he asks.

I nod sharply.

He explores me with his hand, sliding his fingers through my folds, touching my clit with his thumb, pushing one, then two fingers inside me. Learning how I respond.

It's almost unbearably intimate.

I am reminded of why I haven't had sex in more than three years; it's because of this intimacy. But I craved it, and I couldn't deny myself this pleasure forever.

I tell myself it'll be okay. I will be okay.

He brushes his lips over mine and kisses me as he continues to finger me. His kiss is devastating in its tenderness, and then he increases the pressure gradually until it's a desperate, open-mouthed kiss.

I make Julian Fong desperate.

He slides off my underwear and continues to touch me with nothing between us, his skin on mine. Tentatively, I wrap my hand around his erection and move up and down. He hisses out a breath. Enjoying his reaction, I use a bit more pressure and do it again.

"Stop." He struggles to get the word out. "I won't last. It's been a while for me, too."

"How long?"

"Eight months."

"Surely that wasn't due to lack of opportunities. Not when you look like this."

The thought of him being with someone else shouldn't bother me. This is just a fling, and he's a thirty-five-year-old man—I know there have been many others.

But the thought of him being so close to another woman makes me ache.

"I guess...I was waiting for you," he murmurs, and my chest aches in a completely different way.

He removes his fingers from inside me and runs them over my stomach, to my breast. They're wet from my moisture. He rests his chest on top of mine, and I feel so connected to him.

"I missed this," I say, pushing a hand through his short hair. "I missed this so much."

"You shouldn't deprive yourself. In fact, I won't allow it."

"You won't?"

"No. You should be in my bed as much as possible."

He rocks his hips against mine, his erection pressing between my legs, and I moan from the contact *there* and everywhere else.

"Didn't I tell you," he says, "the bedroom is the one place where I already know how to have fun?"

He slides down the bed until his head is between my legs. One thing I remember, from my long-ago sexual experience, is that I love being licked and touched at the same time. But I don't have to tell him. Two fingers penetrate me before his tongue circles my clit.

It's too much, but at the same time, it's not enough.

He licks me skillfully and slides his fingers in and out, and I'm spiraling toward a peak so much higher than what I can reach by myself. I'm almost there, almost there...

I cry out and shake uncontrollably. He continues to lick me through my climax, gradually slowing down until I put my hand on his shoulder to stop him.

When I'm alone, one is always enough. But with him, it's just the beginning.

He kisses his way up my body, over my stomach, taking my left nipple into his mouth and then my right, until he gets to my mouth.

"You're perfect," he says simply.

My body tingles with anticipation as he reaches inside the bedside table and produces a condom. He sits up to roll it on.

"How would you like it?" he asks. "Do you want to be on top?"

I shake my head. I don't want to be the one in control of the rhythm. I want to surrender to whatever he wants to give me.

"You on top," I say.

He settles himself above me and rubs his sheathed cock over my folds. When he starts to push inside, I inhale sharply. It's been a while, and he's thicker than the men I've been with before.

"It's okay," he says. "I know you can take me."

He pushes the rest of the way inside but doesn't start thrusting yet. Instead, he keeps his hips still while he kisses my neck and shoulders. I'm not used to having something so large inside me but, God, it feels good. It feels right.

Slowly, he starts to move, and I wrap my legs around his waist and tighten my hold on him. Julian will keep me safe.

"I've got you," he murmurs. "I've got you."

We move together at a slow but steady pace, and each time he pushes inside me, it feels like he's making me whole. I wrap my arms around his powerful back muscles and keep his skin pressed against mine.

"You feel amazing," he says with wonder.

"You're amazing, too," I whisper.

Nothing can compare to this.

How did I go without it for so long?

He picks up his pace, and I start climbing toward another orgasm. His cock inside me—that's all I need to come. I tip over the edge and cry out. "Oh, oh, oh."

Julian is right behind me, groaning as he reaches his climax.

As I come down from the height of my pleasure, I feel like I'm falling. He pulls out of me, but he's still got me, holding me close and burying his face in my shoulder.

A few minutes later, he goes to the washroom and disposes of the condom, but then he's next to me, pulling me against him, both of us still slick with sweat, both of us still naked.

I feel giddy and my body is mush. "We should do that again sometime."

He chuckles in my ear. "We will." He brushes my hair back and presses a kiss behind my ear. "If there's anything you want, you just tell me. If you want to scream, please feel free to do so."

"Don't worry. I won't hold myself back with you." I mean for it to sound playful, but my tone isn't right—it sounds like it's imbued with deeper meaning.

He strokes my hair. "I hope you're not planning to return to your room now."

"Of course not. I hope you're not planning to pull out that stupid report you were looking at yesterday."

He laughs. "I'll wait until you fall asleep before I start working."

I swat him.

His lips slide to my neck and he kisses me before saying, "I'm at your service whenever you want. Feel free to wake me up if you need me."

And then he falls asleep.

FRIDAY MORNING, I wake up with Courtney in my bed for the second day in a row.

We've spent most of the past thirty-six hours naked, aside from when she was at work yesterday. Those nine hours seemed interminable. All day, I could think of nothing but what I would do to her when she got home, and when she finally returned, we practically attacked each other in the front hall, then had sex on the couch.

And then we had sex in the shower.

And then we ate dinner because sex marathons make a person hungry.

It's been a very good thirty-six hours, I must say.

"Good morning," she says groggily. "Do I really have to go to the lab today?"

"You mumbled something about an important meeting at ten o'clock, so, yes, I think you do. But there's no reason you need to go to work until then, is there?"

She giggles. "You're such a bad influence."

"Me?" I pretend to be horrified. "A bad influence? Surely you're joking."

I roll on top of her and start kissing my way down her body.

By the time she leaves for work at nine thirty, she's had three orgasms and I'm feeling rather pleased with myself.

I head up to the rooftop patio with a book, and because it's a warm summer's day—and because I've become very bad at wearing clothes in the past thirty-six hours—I take off my shirt.

Before I crack open the novel, I spend ten minutes looking at the Toronto skyline. I liked the view when I first looked at this place three years ago, but it didn't take me long to get accustomed to it. Now, thanks to Courtney, I feel like I'm seeing everything with fresh eyes. Admiring the view I've seen so many times before, appreciating the luxury of having a rooftop patio all to myself.

I read a couple chapters, although I'm struggling to keep my eyes open.

I shouldn't be tired. It's still morning and I got at least seven hours of sleep last night, but it's just so peaceful up here above the city. There's a light breeze and the lake glitters in the distance…

I put down my book and close my eyes.

"Is he asleep? But it's eleven o'clock in the morning. He can't be asleep. In a lounge chair. On his patio. It's just not possible."

"I said you wouldn't believe your eyes, didn't I?"

"You did. And I was picturing something…well, to be honest, I pictured something that was wearing a shirt."

Dear God, my brothers are here, ruining my peace. Elena must have let them in while I was getting reacquainted with naptime, something I haven't done in decades. According to my mother, I stopped napping when I was six months old. Why do my brothers have to—

Wait a second.

Brothers. Plural. I heard both of them.

I open my eyes. Cedric is peering at me as though I'm an exotic bird he's never encountered before.

"Cedric!" I say, leaping to my feet. "You're back in Toronto. Since when?"

"Since yesterday."

I give him a hug.

Vince and Cedric give each other a look.

"What?" I say. "What have I done this time?"

"That was an uncharacteristically enthusiastic greeting," Cedric says.

"I haven't seen you since Christmas. Of course I gave you an enthusiastic greeting. Where have you been?"

Cedric and Vince glance at each other again.

"Well, that answers my question about how things are going with Courtney." Vince slaps me on the shoulder. "You're getting laid now, aren't you?"

I did not realize I was so transparent.

"There's a woman?" Cedric asks.

"There is," Vince says. "He's very clear that she's not his girlfriend, but they're living together, so…"

"She's helping me learn to enjoy life." I gesture to the umbrella above me and the book on the table. "I'm paying her five thousand dollars to teach me to enjoy the two-week vacation that my family forced me to take."

"Ah. You're not *willingly* taking a holiday. I should have known."

Well, I guess "forced" isn't quite the right word. I would have gone back to work already if I hadn't realized they had a point. I don't let my family boss me around *that* much.

The break has been good for me, though.

"He does seem to be making the most of it," Vince says.

"He does," Cedric agrees.

I glare at them. "Will you stop talking about me like I'm not here?"

"Fine, fine." Apparently deciding I've spoiled his fun, Vince heads downstairs, leaving me and Cedric alone.

"Where did you go?" I ask.

"Malaysia, Singapore, Thailand, China, Australia, New Zealand, and Fiji."

"Have a good time?"

"I did, but…"

"You're still not writing?"

"I'm writing," he says. "Sort of. I've started half a dozen projects, but I never get beyond the third chapter. Everything I write is complete shit."

"I doubt it."

"No, really."

"Aren't first drafts supposed to be shitty?"

"Not *this* shitty." He runs a hand through his hair.

"What are you going to do now?"

He sighs. "I don't know, but let's not talk about me. You're the one who's sun tanning in the middle of a work day."

"You're the one who spent eight months traveling around the world. Surely you have stories to tell me."

But I can see he doesn't want to do that.

Vince bounds up the stairs. "Yep, you're definitely sleeping with Courtney. I went to your bedroom for a little reconnaissance work, and I saw her suitcase, as well as a strip of condoms on your bedside table. Not inside. On top."

I glare at him. "Stop going through my stuff."

"I didn't have to go through anything. I observed it all from the doorway."

I give him the middle finger.

"On a scale of one to ten," Vince says, "how spectacular is the sex?"

"None of your business," I snap.

"Hmm." Vince strokes his chin. "Cedric, do you think that's a ten? Or maybe an eleven?"

"You've got to be kidding me," I mutter.

"You're starting to sound like your usual self." Cedric pats me on the back. "I was a little worried I'd returned to an alternate universe. When do I get to meet this woman?"

"She met Mom and Po Po on Monday," Vince says. "She returned from work at four o'clock. So, if we stick around for another five hours…"

"Absolutely not," I say. "No way are you two sticking around that long. I can't handle it. Plus, Courtney's working until six since she didn't get in until ten this morning."

"And why would that be?" Vince smirks. "Any particular reason she was late getting to work, lover boy?"

An image of her naked body arched across my bed immediately comes to mind.

I turn to Cedric. "Actually, you're welcome to stick around and have a beer. It's been a while. But I can't handle any more of Vince. He's already been here several times this week. In fact, he tried to drag me to an orgy last Friday."

Cedric shakes his head. "I won't last until four o'clock. I'm pretty jetlagged. I'll see you again sometime next week, okay?"

I admit, I'm a touch disappointed he's leaving so soon.

"Oh!" Vince says. "I almost forgot the other thing I noticed in your bedroom. Joey the Phallic Cactus now has a prime seat by your window. How long has he been there?"

"A phallic cactus," Cedric says. "Is this a cactus that looks like a dick or a strange term for a studded dildo?"

"Joey is a real cactus," Vince says. "Lots of potential for symbolism, don't you think? You could put a phallic cactus in your next book and give me credit for the idea. Ooh! Maybe the phallic cactus could start talking. How about that?"

"Your ideas are crap," Cedric mutters, and I sympathize with him. "How many times have I told you that?

"Two dozen, perhaps?" Vince says cheerfully. "I've lost count. Anyway, you're jetlagged, and I bet Julian wants to fantasize about his new girlfriend while he's sun tanning. As for me, there's always hookers and blow, even at eleven in the morning." He gives me a mock salute before heading downstairs, Cedric behind him.

I sit back down and massage my temples.

As I'm picking up my novel, I realize I didn't correct Vince when he referred to Courtney as my girlfriend.

[17]
COURTNEY

ON FRIDAYS I have lunch with Bethany, a post doc in the lab next to mine. We either go out for sushi or banh mi. Today we're having the latter.

"How's your son?" I ask as we walk to the restaurant.

Bethany has a two-year-old who seems allergic to the idea of sitting still for more than two seconds.

"I got him to eat broccoli last night," she says. "It's a miracle. Of course, it was in between running around with a box on his head and dumping Duplo all over the floor."

Now that I'm in my thirties, most people my age are settling down and having kids, and they often aren't available to go out on Friday and Saturday nights. Though I'm happy to go to their houses and hang out with their kids and try not to swear, it's not the same as when I was younger. It's harder to avoid spending the weekend alone, something which isn't great for my mental health.

But this weekend and next weekend, I have Julian.

Bethany and I reach the banh mi place on Yonge and place our orders. Pork belly for me, as always. We're lucky to get a seat by the window, but before Bethany unwraps her sandwich, she pulls her blonde hair back in a ponytail and looks at me curiously.

"Something's different about you," she says. "I'm not sure what, but something is definitely different."

When we had sushi together last Friday, I hadn't even met Julian yet. I'd admired him from a distance at Chris's Coffee Shop, but that was all.

So much has changed since then.

I have a bite of my delicious sandwich. "You're never going to believe what happened."

I tell her about meeting Julian and our deal and moving in with him. She hasn't heard of his family before, but penthouse-owning CEO gets the point across. I also mention that we've started sleeping together.

When I finish my story, she looks at me with wide eyes.

"Wow," she says. "*Wow*. This is actually happening to *my* friend. When do I get to meet this man of yours? And does he have any hot friends?"

"He has a brother who made a fortune selling his tech start-up, but last time I checked, you were still married."

"Details, details." Bethany waves this off as though it's not important, and we laugh. "What's going to happen when the two weeks are over?"

"It's just a fling. When the two weeks are over, it's over."

She raises her eyebrows. "Is it?"

"Yes," I say. "It is."

I wake up at four in the morning, Julian asleep beside me. This is my third night in his bed. The past two nights, I didn't think about the future at all. I just focused on the present, on having great sex for the first time in years.

Now, perhaps because of my conversation with Bethany, I

think about what will happen at the end of next weekend. I told myself I deserve some fun, which is true, but I also told myself it would be easy to get over him, even if there were pesky feelings involved.

I climb out of bed and head to his en suite washroom, where we've already had sex twice. When I make my way back through the dark bedroom, I trip on something and fall to the floor.

"Ow," I groan, but quietly, so I don't wake Julian.

I hurt my right foot on a piece of furniture; no big deal. Since it's only my third night here, I don't have the layout of the room perfectly memorized.

I stay on the floor, wrap my hands around my foot, and rock back and forth. I'll be okay. A minute or two, and the pain will subside.

When I feel better, I hobble to the bed and get under the covers.

It's okay, I tell myself. *You'll be just fine.*

But I'm wide awake now.

Twenty minutes later, I get up and head to the window. I look out at the cityscape before me. So many bright lights, so many people, and I'm all the way up here, with just my thoughts to keep me company.

There's a lump in my throat, and it's suddenly painful to swallow. The view before me is pretty and I loved it when I first saw it, but in a way, it's so, so sad. In a city of millions of people, there are so many of us who are alone. Although I'm not alone tonight, this is just a temporary break from reality.

A few tears slide silently down my cheeks.

As the years go by, I'll watch things happen to those around me but stay apart from it all. I know this is how it has to be. I've known for a while; it's nothing new. But I can't lie to myself. Sometimes I fantasize that Julian and I could have more than a couple weeks together.

Impossible fantasies.

I can't keep waking up in his bed and cuddling with him before I start my day. I need to preserve a little distance so those feelings don't become more than they already are.

I take one more look at Julian before walking back to the guest room and climbing into the bed I haven't used for a few nights.

I can't have the same things as other people.

Sure, I can have a job, I can enjoy gingerbread lattes, and I can be a decent friend—as long as I don't subject my friends to the darkness inside me—but...

God, why do I have to be so *stupid*?

I couldn't finish university on the first try.

And will I really be able to hold onto this job, or am I destined to fuck that up, too?

I can see the next year laid out clearly before me. I see the lows I will reach...except I don't see the bottom of them, don't know exactly how low I will go. It's fucking terrifying.

I know I'll lose interest in the world around me, including my research. But I can't see exactly how much gray fog I'll be pushing through, or how dead I'll feel inside, or how impossibly heavy my chest will feel when I try to breathe.

It could be worse than last time.

That's the thing about life. It can *always* get worse.

More tears build up behind my eyes, but I feel too disconnected to actually cry. I want to cry, because when I'm in this state, my best hope of sleeping is exhausting myself from crying. There have been weeks when I cried myself to sleep every night, and there have been weeks when I was too numb to cry but desperately wanted to.

Finally, the tears fall, and finally, I sleep.

When I wake up on Saturday morning, there's still a heavy pressure in my chest. My right foot is okay, though. When I press on it, there's a bit of pain, but if you press on anything hard enough, there's going to be pain.

I don't want to get up and face the day. I don't want to fake a smile for Julian.

It's only seven o'clock. I can stay in bed for a while.

I force myself to take a few deep breaths. In and out. In and out. Unlike last night, my thoughts aren't spiraling out of control. Later, I'll call Naomi. That will be good for me. A nice walk will be good for me, too, as will brushing my teeth, taking a shower, and putting on a cute outfit. Today isn't going to be a great day, but I should be able to stop it from being a truly awful day with a little self-care. It would be better if I were at my apartment, because then I wouldn't have to worry about Julian, though at the same time, it'll be good for me to socialize.

I think tripping on Julian's dresser last night was what set me off. Sometimes the stupidest things get to me, like trying to turn on my laptop and discovering the battery is dead. That's made me cry inconsolably before.

And yet when my grandmother died last year, I was okay. I mean, I was sad and bereaved, and I knew that feeling would last a while, but somehow it felt bearable.

I am a freak.

Shh, I tell myself. *You're okay.*

The morning light filters in through the blinds. Sometimes that would make me smile, but not today. Maybe tomorrow. It's August, and my once-every-five-years episodes of depression usually don't begin until late September or October, so I should still have several more good weeks, punctuated by the occasional bad day.

"Courtney?" It's Julian. He's standing in the doorway, frowning. "Why are you in the guest room?"

It's early and my brain isn't functional enough to come up

with a compelling lie. "I wasn't feeling great, so I came here in the middle of the night."

"Are you coming down with something? Do you have a fever? A sore throat?" His eyebrows knit together, and his concern is touching. "Do you need to go to the doctor?"

I sit up and shake my head. "No fever or anything. I'm just... not feeling great."

I wait for him to ask for clarification. He opens his mouth, then shuts it. Opens his mouth, then shuts it again. Julian likes answers, and he likes to fix problems.

But he doesn't ask, perhaps sensing I don't want to talk about it. Instead, he crawls into bed with me and curls his body around me from behind.

He's just holding me, nothing more, and there's something lovely about being held, especially by Julian. A person's touch is so simple, yet it can mean so much. It won't make last night go away, but it makes me feel a little better. A little less alone, even if it's only temporary. I'm still tender and vulnerable, but I can feel myself getting stronger with each breath.

"If you'd prefer to be by yourself, I can leave," he says.

I burrow against him. "No, I want you to stay."

He holds me closer and wraps his leg over mine so I'm completely surrounded by him. It almost feels like he could make everything go away, make me whole again, turn me into a person who doesn't fall to pieces because her laptop isn't charged. Or because she tripped over a piece of furniture or knocked a pile of books off her desk. Even Julian Fong is not that powerful, but he's still good for my mental health right now, and I'll take what he's giving me.

He's also getting aroused.

"Ignore that," he says when I rub back against him. "I'm sorry, I can't help it when I'm with you. We certainly don't need to do anything now." He pauses. "How about I make you breakfast in bed? What would you like?"

I almost feel like crying, but it's different from last night. He's so sweet to me.

"I liked your eggs and bacon last weekend," I tell him, trying to keep my voice from cracking. "But don't go. Not yet."

We stay curled up in bed for a few more minutes before I let him prepare breakfast for me. The kitchen is a long way from the bedrooms, so I don't smell the bacon or hear the banging of pots and pans. I just relax into the mattress and try not to think too hard. Focus on my senses and not what's going on in my poor brain. Elena has replaced the duvet cover since the last time I slept in this room. It's pastel-colored with flowers, and it's quite pretty. I run my fingers over it.

Julian returns with a wooden tray that has little legs on the bottom. There's a plate full of bacon and eggs and toast, as well as two lattes.

"You have a special breakfast-in-bed tray?" I ask.

"I have everything."

I laugh. "This is too much food for me."

"I know. You're supposed to share." He picks up a piece of bacon and holds it to my lips.

I take a bite. "You make it crispy, not chewy. That's the correct way to cook bacon but my sister disagrees." I pick up another piece of bacon and start feeding it to Julian. I inhale sharply when he licks the salt and grease off my fingers. "Are we going to feed each other scrambled eggs like this, too?"

He takes a piece of scrambled egg and holds it to my mouth. I laugh again before eating it. This is definitely the first time anyone has fed me scrambled eggs with their fingers. Actually, it's the first time anyone has brought me breakfast in bed.

Soon, we start using forks like normal people. Everything tastes good, but because I'm not quite myself right now, I don't enjoy it as much as the breakfast he made me last weekend. Still, I'm enjoying it a little.

When we're finished eating, Julian puts the tray aside and we sit in bed with our lattes.

"What would you like to do today?" he asks. "Anything you like. Anything at all."

"Paris?"

"If you can take a few days off work—"

I put a hand to his chest. "I forgot who I was talking to. That was a joke. What I really want is…"

I STARE at the baby in the monster onesie. Five minutes ago, she was screaming like, well, a monster, but now she's sleeping peacefully in Courtney's arms.

We're in a townhome in the east end with Courtney's family. There's her brother, Jeremy, and his wife, Lydia, as well as her sister, Naomi, and Naomi's boyfriend, Will. And Jeremy and Lydia's baby.

When I asked Courtney what she wanted to do today, she said she wanted to visit her baby niece. She didn't expect me to go with her, but I offered to. I joked that if she left me alone, I'd probably end up going to the office. That's not true, though. I just want to be by her side, since she seemed a bit off this morning.

I don't know much about babies. Neither of my brothers have children, and I only have two cousins, and they don't have children, either. This baby is admittedly cute, and Courtney seems quite taken with her, so I'm glad we're here because I like seeing Courtney smile.

Now that Baby Heather is asleep, everyone's attention turns to me.

"So, you're dating my sister," Jeremy says.

"Yes." I keep it simple, rather than explaining the whole story. From what Courtney's told me, her sister knows the details, but her brother doesn't.

"Be careful," Will says. "He tried to punch me in the face for doing that."

Naomi gives Will a playful shove.

"It's interesting," Jeremy muses. "Courtney hasn't brought anyone to meet her family in a long time, and then suddenly she shows up with *you*. I know who you are, Julian."

That sounds ominous. I'm not sure what to say.

"You're a playboy," Jeremy says. "Every week, you've got a new woman. You're rich, so you can get away with treating women like crap. And now you want to fuck with my sister?"

Oh boy.

"Stop the overprotective brother routine." Courtney glares at him.

"Besides," Naomi says, "you've got it wrong. Julian's brother is the playboy who posed semi-nude in a calendar. Not him."

Jeremy frowns at this new piece of information. "Right."

"Don't worry," I say. "I have every intention of treating your sister well and zero intention of posing nude in a calendar."

"You know what you should do?" Naomi says. "Since you have so much money..."

"Naomi!" Courtney hisses.

"You should take my sister to Paris."

"I offered," I say.

Naomi turns to Courtney. "Then why aren't you in Paris right now?"

"Because I can't take a week off work with only one or two days' notice."

Naomi groans. "You're no fun."

"How about we go away next weekend?" I suggest. "You won't have to miss work, or maybe an afternoon at the most."

"To Paris? No. The flight will consume almost the entire weekend—"

"Not to Paris." I consider the options. "Montreal?"

"Yes!" Naomi says. "You should totally go to Montreal together. Julian, you should give her a credit card so she can buy a new wardrobe for the trip. Like in *Pretty Woman*. You should take advantage of your rich companion while you have him, Courtney. One more week until..." She puts her hand over her mouth.

"One week until what?" Jeremy asks.

Courtney gives Naomi a dirty look. "You weren't supposed to say anything."

"What am I missing here?" Jeremy narrows his eyes at me.

Well, this is going to be fun.

Courtney bites her lip. "Julian's family wanted him to take two weeks off work because he's a stressed-out workaholic, and he hired me to be a companion of sorts for those two weeks. To teach him how to have fun."

"Is he paying you to be a *prostitute*?" Jeremy starts to stand up, but Lydia pulls him back down.

"It's not like that at all," Courtney says. "I see why you'd think that, and Naomi's mention of *Pretty Woman* probably didn't help, and Julian and I, we did... But it's not like that."

"I *knew* it," Naomi says. "I knew the reason you hadn't talked to me for a few days was because you were busy having sex."

Courtney's cheeks turn red, and I can feel mine getting warm, too. I'm about to open my mouth to say something—although what would make this situation less awkward, I have no idea—when Heather starts wailing. For some reason, Courtney thrusts her into my arms, though of the six adults in this room, I must be the worst person to take care of a baby.

"Shh." I awkwardly pat Heather's back. "Shh."

Courtney marches over to Jeremy. "Why do you have to play

overprotective brother now, when I'm thirty-one? Where were you ten years ago, hmm? Where were you when I was...when I was..." She looks back at me. There must be something she doesn't want to say in my presence. I debate leaving the room, but I also don't want to leave her. Plus, I have a baby in my hands. "...when I really needed someone else on my side? When Dad didn't believe anything I said? You know he takes you seriously and listens to you more than me and Naomi. You could have helped then, but you didn't. That was when I needed a big brother. That was the time to interfere in my life. Not now. I'm fine on my own now, and Julian treats me well. So, please. Just stop it. I don't want to have to worry about what stupid thing you're going to freak out about next."

The room is quiet except for Heather, who is crying softly. I bounce her up and down, and she seems to like that. She rubs her little hand all over my face.

I don't know what happened ten years ago, but I'm angry at Jeremy for not being there when Courtney needed him. If he doesn't apologize, I'll happily give him shit, too.

He rests his elbows on his knees and looks down. "You're right," he says softly. "I think I've been trying to make up for it, but I can't, and I'm sorry."

Courtney swallows. "Okay. That's... Thank you for saying that."

He stands up and gives her a hug, and she squeezes him tight. He says something quietly in her ear. It sounds like, "It'll be better this time."

Jeremy sits down, and Courtney cuddles up beside me. Nobody says anything for a minute, until Heather lets out a high-pitched scream and I realize I've stopped bouncing her.

Lydia comes over to me. "I'll take her. I think she needs to be changed." She disappears upstairs with her daughter.

"Well," Naomi says as the tension in the room starts to dissi-pate. "What was I saying before? Courtney, I really think you two should go to Montreal together. Maybe Julian has a private jet you can take?"

I stop myself from rolling my eyes. "I do not have a private jet. Terrible waste of money, and I'm not a billionaire. We'll fly on Porter from the island airport. If that's what Courtney wants." I place my hand on her back. "What do you think?"

She nods. "Sounds good. We can go Friday after work and come back Sunday evening."

"Excellent. I'll make the arrangements."

I've been to Montreal many times before, but I've never been with Courtney, and that will be a completely different experience. A good way to end my two-week vacation. I start to think of all the places we can have sex in the hotel room, then remember I'm surrounded by her family, including her big brother.

"Don't worry," I say to Jeremy. "I'll take good care of your sister. You have my word. I don't blame you for being concerned. If I had a sister, I'd probably feel the same."

He nods in acknowledgement.

I mean it. I would never do anything to hurt her.

"I still think Courtney deserves a new wardrobe for this trip," Naomi says.

"Naomi!" Courtney says. "Stop trying to make Julian throw money at me."

I withdraw a credit card from my wallet. "Here. Buy a nice dress for when we go out in Montreal."

She doesn't take the card. "I don't need to recreate scenes from movies just to please my sister."

I look at her for a moment, trying to figure out what she really wants, if it really would make her happy to shop for a new dress.

I press the credit card into her hand. "Just one dress, and a pair of shoes to go with it." I brush her hair back from her ear and whisper, "Something that makes you feel sexy."

"Okay."

"I'm coming on this shopping trip," Naomi announces.

"Of course you are," Courtney says. "I have no idea where to go."

I touch her shoulder. "You can also get the mani-pedi you were talking about the other day. You and your sister, if you want."

Naomi turns to me. "I think you should stick around for more than a week. Not because you're rich and can pay for my manicures—"

"Hey," Will says. "I can pay for manicures."

"Ooh! Do you want to come with me? I think it would be so much fun to go to the nail salon together."

"Absolutely not." He folds his arms over his chest.

"Julian volunteered to go with me, actually," Courtney says.

"Did he?" Jeremy lifts his eyebrows.

Right. I did. To be honest, Courtney could get me to do pretty much anything. Better for her to go to the salon with her sister, though.

Lydia comes downstairs with Heather and hands her back to Courtney, who kisses the baby's forehead. Heather sticks her arm out and nearly pokes me in the eye, then decides she's more interested in Courtney's nose.

"Remember," Courtney says to Heather. "I'm Aunt Courtney. Your *fun* auntie."

I can't help it. Seeing Courtney with a baby sets off some unexpected feelings inside me.

My mother and grandmother would be pleased.

"TRY THIS ONE!" Naomi thrusts a black cocktail dress in my direction.

I glance at the price tag. "It's three hundred dollars."

She gives me a look.

Right. Julian wouldn't mind me spending three hundred dollars on a dress. It's pocket change to him.

He told me the pin number for his "emergency" credit card. I wonder what his limit is. It's probably something ridiculous. I asked him how much I was allowed to spend, and he wouldn't give me a number, but after I bugged him enough, he said a thousand dollars for the dress and shoes...and jewelry, if I want it. So three hundred dollars is fine.

My sister and I are at a dress boutique on Queen Street. We've already been to a couple stores, but I didn't find anything I liked.

I examine the black cocktail dress. "Okay. I'll try it."

"Wait. This one's better." She shoves another black dress into my hands. It has off-the-shoulder sleeves and flares out at the bottom.

I head to the change room with the two black dresses. The first one is too tight.

This is what I hate about clothes shopping. It makes me feel self-conscious about my appearance and my weight, though I'm not as bothered by that today as I often am when I'm shopping. I just remind myself of how Julian responds to my body, and it's easy to restore my confidence.

The next dress is significantly better. I leave the change room to show Naomi.

"I love it," she says.

When I spin around, the skirt flies up more than expected. I quickly shove it down. "So do I. I'm going to get it."

After leaving the dress boutique, we head to a shoe store and get me some strappy black shoes. Then we meet Lydia at a nail salon on Yonge Street.

I show her the dress, and she tells me it's lovely. Then she pulls out her phone. "I wonder how Jeremy is doing with Heather."

This is her first time away from Heather for more than an hour. She's getting her nails done, and then she's heading right back home. Naomi invited her to come dress shopping, too, but she said no.

"I'm sure he's fine," Naomi says.

"What if she's been crying the whole time?"

We can't stop Lydia from texting Jeremy, who replies with a picture of Heather sitting in his lap, no tears in sight. Then we pick our nail polish colors and are led to comfy chairs at the back, where we submerge our feet in warm water.

"Oh my God," Lydia groans. "This is so nice."

We're quiet for a minute before Naomi turns to me and says, "So you're sleeping with Julian. What's he like in bed?"

"I'm not answering that question," I say, but I can't help a smile from crossing my lips.

It's Tuesday now, so we've been sleeping together for almost a week. I've had more sex in the past week than I had in the ten years before it, and it's pretty phenomenal sex.

But I'm not saying that out loud in a nail salon.

"Fine." Naomi sticks up her nose. "Keep secrets from your favorite sister. See if I care."

"You're my only sister."

"So tell your only sister what he looks like without a shirt, since he refuses to pose naked for a charity calendar."

"He, um, works out every day and hardly has any body fat. So, uh. He looks very good. Like he could be a model."

And I'm sleeping with him. It's still hard to wrap my head around.

"Lydia…" I trail off as I glance over at my sister-in-law and see that she's asleep. I bet she's seriously sleep-deprived, thanks to Heather.

I'm a touch sleep-deprived too, since Julian and I were fooling around until midnight, and there was some sex in the middle of the night, too.

"You really like him, don't you?" Naomi says.

I'm not sure how to reply. "He's nice, and he's essentially paying me to have fun."

I wonder what the other women in the nail salon think of me now.

"Forget the money," she says. "You're falling for him, aren't you?"

Julian's definitely gotten to me a little. I like him, and I'm getting a bit attached…but I'm not falling in love. Although it won't be easy to go back to my regular life after this, I know I can do it. I have to do it.

I shake my head.

"Bullshit," Naomi declares.

Lydia awakes with a start. "Bullshit? What's bullshit? Damn, that was a nice nap."

"You were out for all of three minutes," I say. "Hardly a nap."

"I'll take what I can get. What were you talking about?"

"Naomi insists I'm falling in love with Julian. She said 'bullshit' when I denied it."

"Of course you're falling in love with him," Lydia says. "What woman wouldn't? And didn't he look cute with Heather?"

"He did," Naomi agrees. "You should make babies together."

"I've known him for less than two weeks," I say. "We are not making babies together."

However…

I once read a book where the heroine's ovaries twitched whenever she saw her crush playing with a child, holding a baby, or washing dishes. I rolled my eyes and thought it was ridiculous, but my ovaries may have twitched when I saw him with my niece.

I need to give my ovaries a stern talking-to.

Naomi turns to the woman who's massaging her feet. "My sister's sleeping with a CEO. He doesn't have a private jet, but he has a penthouse and a… Courtney, what kind of car does he drive?"

"I have no idea. I presume he owns a car, but I've never seen him drive."

"Well, anyway, he's so rich that he has a nice car drive him around all the time, and he gave my sister his credit card…"

"What's his name?" the woman asks. "If he's a CEO, maybe I've heard of him."

"Julian Fong."

I shake my head in despair. Now the entire nail salon knows who I'm sleeping with. Multiple women are looking in our direction.

The older woman on the chair across from me says, "I know his company. My husband has them handle his investments. And I just read in the paper that his family is funding a new cardiology wing at a hospital in Markham."

The woman next to me says, "I've seen pictures of him before, and…*damn*."

"Are you his mistress?" the older woman asks.

"No, I'm just—"

"Not that I'm judging. Nothing wrong with that, as long as he treats you right. In the romances novels I've read…"

The chatter continues, and I try not to turn as red as a watermelon.

"Okay, okay," Naomi finally says. "I think this is embarrassing Courtney a little more than I'd intended. Let's, um, talk about something else! Anyone seen any good movies lately?"

Naomi eventually manages to drag the conversation away from me and Julian, but I continue to think about him.

I'm not in love with him, but he makes my pesky ovaries twitch.

And other parts of me, too, if I'm being honest.

When I get to Julian's, he greets me at the door with a tie in his hand.

"I have a surprise for you." He turns me around so he can blindfold me with the tie.

I giggle. "Does this surprise involve sex?"

"That will come later, but for now…"

He takes my hand. We head up a set of stairs, so I know we're going to the rooftop patio, and soon I feel a light breeze on my skin. He guides me into a chair before pulling off the blindfold.

In front of me is a table for two with salad, bread, olive oil, and a bottle of white wine chilling in an ice bucket. Julian sits down across from me. He's wearing a purple dress shirt, the top button undone, and he looks incredibly sexy.

And he prepared dinner for me. On his rooftop patio.

It's not quite dark yet, but the sun is sinking in the sky, and it's just the two of us, high above the city.

"Oh!" I exclaim. "This is amazing."

"You haven't tasted it yet."

"Everything you do is amazing."

It's true. Julian doesn't do anything by half measures.

The green salad has fresh figs, goat cheese, and a simple vinaigrette, and it does, indeed, taste delicious. I break off a piece of bread, dip it in the olive oil, and pop it into my mouth.

"Oh my God," I groan. "This is incredible. Did you bake it?"

"I'm not *that* talented."

"I suspect you'll prove otherwise in the bedroom tonight."

I haven't talked freely about sex in years, but with Julian, it's easy.

And he really is that talented. In the bedroom…and elsewhere. I'm sure he could bake bread this delicious if he gave it a try. Lack of experience never seems to stop him; his lemon squares, for example, were divine.

He takes my hand, his touch sending tingles to parts of my body that are *not* my ovaries, and examines my red nail polish. "How was your shopping trip?"

"Successful. Don't peek in the garment bag. I want it to be a surprise, but let me assure you, it's *very* sexy."

He looks at me with a smoldering gaze. "Did you get shoes?"

"I did. Also very sexy."

"Did you spend a lot of my money?"

"Including the manicures and pedicures for three people? It was…" I do some quick math. "Close to eight hundred dollars." I put a hand to my mouth. "Wow."

He laughs. "Courtney, it's fine."

"You gave me your credit card and pin number. You must really trust me."

"I do."

We are quiet for a minute and focus on eating our salads. It's a simple salad with only a few ingredients—but they are quality ingredients, plus Julian made it for me, and we are sitting outside as the sun sets.

This is perfect. I don't want to forget this moment. Ever.

"Your reaction proves why I trust you with my credit card," he says. "You would feel too guilty to spend a significant amount of money."

"Eight hundred dollars is a significant amount."

"It's nothing. If it makes you happy…"

"A seventy-five-cent pineapple bun can make me happy."

"And I like that about you."

He takes away our empty salad bowls and goes downstairs to get more food. I sip my wine and look around. It won't be a dazzling sunset, but there are still a few brushstrokes of pale orange and pink in the sky, and I feel like it's just for us.

Our main course is sausage ragout over polenta.

"Would you like some fresh pepper?" he asks.

"Sure."

He brings out the most enormous pepper grinder I have ever seen. Seriously, it's gigantic. I wonder if he bought it just for this occasion. It puts Joey the Phallic Cactus to shame.

"Fortunately," I say, "I know you're not compensating for anything."

We laugh together.

Perhaps he bought it just to make me laugh.

"Parmesan?" he asks.

I nod and he grates some on top of my food.

The food is tasty like I knew it would be, and as the sky darkens, Julian lights a couple of candles in the middle of the table. He's very good at planning a romantic night.

You don't deserve this, a little voice whispers inside my head.

I push it away. It's just one night. Why shouldn't I have this?

But it's not just one night. I've spent a week and a half with Julian, and I've had a wonderful time. He's an incredibly thoughtful man.

Not to mention, I'm being paid for this. I'll get a trip to New York *and* a trip to Montreal out of it.

I don't deserve it, but somehow, I have it anyway. It's like a modern fairy tale, even though fairy tales don't come true for people like me. There are some things I just can't have because of who I am.

I pick up a forkful of polenta and ragout. It no longer tastes right, and when I swallow, it's almost painful. I try to smile as I reach for my wine glass, not wanting Julian to notice anything's off.

What kind of woman gets depressed in the middle of the most romantic dinner of her life? Something is seriously wrong with me.

I don't deserve this.

It's a good thing it'll be over soon. Next week, I'll be back to my regularly-scheduled life, back to my not-so-luxurious apartment.

Back to not having Julian.

I can't have a relationship with anyone. It's too much of a risk. A relationship could destroy me; it nearly did before. My sister took me to the hospital, and I had to stay there for a week. I had to quit school.

But, God, I'm going to miss him. The thought of being without him causes a tightness in my chest. He's been so good to me, and he deserves better. He deserves romantic nights on his rooftop patio with a better woman.

The thought of that woman is so damn painful, it brings tears to my eyes.

I struggle to feed myself another bite of dinner, and some of the ragout falls on my shirt. Great. Now I have tomato on my white shirt. I can't even feed myself without making a mess like a toddler. I'm an idiot.

"I'll get Elena to take that out for you," Julian says. "She can remove any stain."

"Thank you," I mumble.

Depression washes over me like a giant wave, and I am swept

up in it, unable to stop it. On some level, I know I'm not an idiot for getting my shirt dirty, and why shouldn't I enjoy a nice meal with Julian?

Still, I can't stop thinking otherwise.

Five minutes ago, I was fine, eating delicious food and laughing at the phallic pepper grinder like I didn't have a care in the world.

And now…this.

Julian kneels on the floor beside me and takes my hand. "Are you okay? What's wrong?"

I hate that he's so observant. Or maybe he doesn't have to be observant to see that I'm having a meltdown, because I can't even hide how fucked up I am. I can't do anything right.

Shh. I hear my sister's voice. *You're okay.*

Maybe I should call her.

I have plans for when I get like this, which include calling Naomi, as well as a hot cup of tea, a blanket, a favorite book or movie—some combination of those things. I won't be able to fully enjoy them when I'm in this state, but they'll help ground me.

"I need to be alone right now," I say.

I don't look at Julian; I just get up and hurry down the stairs.

Except apparently I can't even run down the stairs without being a failure. I trip on the second-to-last stair and go flying.

I'M ABOUT to follow Courtney when I hear a loud bang and a shriek.

I rush downstairs. When I see her lying at the bottom of the stairs, not moving, my chest constricts and it feels like I can't breathe. But somehow, my feet get me to her side, and I continue to get oxygen into my lungs.

She's moaning in pain. At least she's conscious. I didn't see what happened—I have no idea how bad her fall was—but she looks awful.

I pull out my phone. "Honey, it's okay," I say, trying to sound calmer than I feel. "I'm calling an ambulance."

She immediately sits up, a terrified look on her face. "The last thing I want to do is deal with paramedics and police officers. Don't call. *Please.*"

Her pleading tone catches me off guard.

"It would make everything worse," she says. "You don't understand."

"You're badly hurt."

"It's not what you think."

To my horror, she gets to her feet. Before I can stop her, she starts walking, and she limps for the first two steps, but that's all.

"It's just a scratch," she tells me.

She walks toward the guest bedroom. I follow. She sits down on the bed and allows me to roll up the bottom of her pants and look at her leg. There's only a small mark.

It doesn't explain anything.

"Before you ran downstairs," I say, "you told me you needed to be alone. What happened? Did I do something wrong?"

"Oh, God." She splays her hands over her face. "Don't make everything about you. The world does not revolve around *you*."

"I just want to understand."

"No, you really don't."

"Talk to me, sweetheart. Tell me what's going on."

"Why are you calling me 'sweetheart'?"

It just popped out of my mouth, but… "I care about you."

I do. As I speak the words, I realize I care about her a lot.

"You wouldn't if you really knew me," she says.

"Tell me," I say gently, "so I can decide for myself."

We look at each other, Courtney sitting on the bed, her face red and blotchy, and me kneeling on the floor beside her.

She starts crying. At first, quiet tears fall down her cheeks, but then she's bawling, sobbing ugly tears, and all of me aches for her. I want to fix it, but I can't fix it if I don't know what's going on. I climb into bed and wrap my arms around her. She buries her face against me and continues to cry.

After a few minutes, her sobs are less frequent, less desperate.

"It's okay." I stroke her back. "You don't have to talk to me." I hate saying those words. I want to demand she tell me exactly what's wrong, but that wouldn't be the right thing to do. "Do you want to call your sister? Do you want me to drive you to a friend's house? I don't think you should be alone now, but you don't have to be with me."

"I don't deserve you," she murmurs.

I can't stand those words.

"You're not thinking clearly," I say, a bit too irritably.

I ease her down so she's lying in the enormous guest bed, and I hold her from behind like I did a few nights ago when I woke up to find her missing from my bedroom. I rub circles over her body.

"It's okay," I say. "I'm here with you."

She releases a shuddering breath and snuggles closer to me.

"I have dessert," I offer. "It's apple crumble that I'm keeping warm in the oven. There's vanilla ice cream, too."

"Maybe later."

"I could get you a gingerbread latte? Or I can make you a regular latte here. Or tea."

She nods against me. "Tea is good. It's on my list."

I'm not sure what she means, but I'm glad to have something to do. "What kind of tea?"

"Whatever you have."

I head to the kitchen and tap my fingers against the counter impatiently as I wait for the electric kettle to boil. Then I make a pot of Earl Grey and bring it to the bedroom on the breakfast tray, along with two teacups. When the tea is ready, I pour us each a cup, and she holds hers just below her nose and breathes in deeply.

"I can't smell it right now," she says glumly, "but I'm sure it's high-quality stuff."

I shrug. "I don't drink a lot of tea. My mom got it for me."

"What do you drink?"

"When I'm working, I have about ten espressos a day."

"Of course you do." She rocks back and forth. "I'm sorry. I'm so sorry."

"Sorry for all the coffee beans that go toward feeding my espresso habit?"

She laughs, but it sounds hollow.

"Are you a little better now?" I ask.

"I'm in control. Sort of. I started to feel depressed when we were eating, and then I completely lost it when I tripped on the stairs, but now…" She looks down. "I'm sorry. None of this is your fault, and I'm sorry you have to deal with me like this." She hesitates. "It's like I have these attacks of depression that come upon me suddenly—I think of them as being similar to panic attacks. It probably sounds weird, but it happens sometimes, and now that it's approaching five years, they're more frequent. Soon, I'll be living in a constant cloud of gray. Every five years, I sink into a deep depression, and I can feel it coming on. I don't know why it recurs on such a predictable schedule, but it does."

I absorb her words, then put down our teacups—it's too hot to drink anyway—and wrap her in my arms again.

"Is this what happened on the weekend, too?"

"Yes, but it wasn't as bad. I think it was worse this time in part because I was trying to keep up a happy front since you went to so much effort to prepare a nice dinner. I appreciate that, I really do. I'm sorry I ruined it."

"You don't need to keep saying 'sorry.' For the next hour, don't apologize to me at all."

She nods. "These thoughts…they keep running through my head, and they're awful. The food you made was delicious, but I stopped being able to taste it properly. Depression isn't like being really sad. Actually, I consider sadness a positive emotion because it's manageable. I don't feel as helpless when I'm sad. It's so much better, you have no idea. Or maybe you do. I shouldn't jump to conclusions."

I shake my head.

I don't know what to do. I'm out of my depth. I just know I want to be here for her.

"I'm sorry," she says again. "This isn't what you signed up for. You wanted someone who knows how to have fun!" She says it with faux cheer. "That's what you're paying me for, and I'm failing miserably at it."

"No more 'sorry,'" I remind her. "And you are not failing. You've done a great job." I pause as something occurs to me. "Ten years ago, when you were in university…"

"That was my worst episode of depression. I had to go on leave during my last year of undergrad, and then my boyfriend dumped me, which didn't help."

I see terror in her eyes as she thinks back to that time.

"There's no trigger," she says. "Everything can be going great and then it just happens. Even in between my bad episodes, I'm not quite normal. I have to be careful. Though usually I'm pretty good at caring for myself."

"Have you tried getting help? There are—"

"Don't," she whispers. "Please don't. That's what everyone asks when they first hear about my depression—not that I tell many people about it. But from what you know of me, do you really think I would have suffered so much without trying to get help?"

"No, but maybe—"

"I've tried everything. I've lost track of how many drugs I've failed to respond to. I've tried therapy, and for whatever reason, that hasn't worked for me, either. I refuse to do ECT—electro-convulsive therapy—because it sounds so damn invasive and because of the cognitive side effects. I know I wouldn't be able to deal with the memory problems. I tried rTMS, and it felt like I was being hit over the head with a hammer for half an hour. Even then, I went back for a second session, but it was no better. They even talked about a study that would involve drilling a hole in my head to implant a pacemaker, but I draw the line at someone drilling a fucking hole in my head."

I don't understand all the things Courtney is talking about, and I make a mental note to look them up tomorrow. I'm not going to ask her to explain more than she already has.

"You said it happens every five years," I say. "It's not chronic. It goes away eventually, but not with the help of drugs or anything else?"

"Sometimes it lasts six months, sometimes well over a year. The one constant is that it goes away after I've given up on treatment, so that's how I know none of those things have worked." She reaches for her teacup. "It's not supposed to be like this. You're supposed to try a few drugs and find one that works. Maybe it won't be the first drug, but you're supposed to find something soon enough. But there are many people like me who have treatment-resistant depression. And if you suggest a little yoga or tai chi will fix it, I will stab you."

"Fair enough."

"Some people think those of us with depression just don't appreciate the little things in life, which you know isn't true for me. Sometimes I wonder if my depression is actually the reason I'm good at that. Every five years, I become incapable of enjoying gourmet ice cream on a hot summer's day and other small pleasures, so when I'm able to enjoy them, it feels like such a gift. In fact, sometimes I think of myself as an innately happy person who suffers from depression." She smiles at me weakly. "I don't want to talk about this anymore."

We drink our tea in silence for a couple of minutes. There are many more things I want to ask, but I keep them to myself.

"Let's watch a movie," I say. "You pick."

She picks *Wedding Crashers* because she wants something that doesn't require much thought. We eat warm apple crumble with vanilla ice cream as we watch the movie, and I'm pleased with myself for baking something so delicious. I went to a local grocer to buy produce today, and I enjoyed looking at the selection of fresh fruits and vegetables. I rarely go grocery shopping—Elena takes care of that for me—and the novelty of it, combined with the way I've been seeing the world through Courtney's eyes lately, made it a pleasurable experience.

Or maybe my baking skills aren't all that impressive. Maybe

the crumble just tastes so good because everything tastes good these days.

Courtney laughs occasionally during the movie, but it's a brittle laughter. She's not quite herself. The thought of her hurting so much causes an unbearable ache inside me; I can't stand to see her suffer. I need to fix this for her. I have resources and contacts that she does not.

I put it on my to-do list for tomorrow, along with planning our trip to Montreal. For some reason, I want to plan the trip myself rather than ask Priya for help. Plus, I have the time to do it.

I ask Courtney if she wants some wine, but she says no, it's probably best if she doesn't drink more tonight. So I make another pot of tea.

When the movie's over, I gather her up in my arms and carry her to my bedroom. She puts on one of my T-shirts for bed, as she's been doing the past few nights. I like seeing her in my clothes.

"It's nice to have you around," she says, running her hand over my face, like she's exploring me. "It helps. It can't solve everything, but it helps."

Five minutes later, she's asleep.

IT'S A NEW DAY, and I'm walking to work. The sun is out, but it's still cool, reminding me that it'll soon be fall. Leaves changing color, pumpkin spice everything. I associate fall with falling into depression because my episodes of severe depression always start at this time of year.

For now, though, I'm mostly okay, though I feel vulnerable and exposed after last night.

I don't like talking about my problems. Some people find it cathartic, but I never have. Plus, it reminds me of the time I told my parents when I was sixteen.

I knew there was something wrong with me, so I starting talking to a guidance counselor at school. She said I was probably depressed, and she insisted I tell my parents and get them to take me to the doctor. I knew my parents would not react well, as I told her again and again. But her only solution to my problem was to tell my parents, and she assured me they'd be understanding. I thought she was full of shit.

And I was right. They did not take it well. My mom acted like it was all my fault, and my dad refused to believe there was any real problem and thought I could just snap out of it.

So I don't like telling people about my problems, though talking to Julian went okay. He listened. He held me. He asked what he could do for me, and he did it. In the end, it was good to have him there, even if I had to patiently explain all my efforts to treat my depression.

Except now I feel like I've cut open my skin and forced him to look at my heart, my kidneys, my liver, and although I've been sewn back up, it'll never be the same again.

It's hard to keep secrets when you're living together. I had to tell him—he deserved to know why I flipped out. But in less than a week, it'll be over, and I'll go back to my regularly-schedule life. It sounds impossible, but that's what will happen.

Two weeks. That's what we agreed on, and it's for the best. Although I've become a bit attached to him, I still think I'll be able to manage.

If I gave him a chance to break me like Dane did, that would be a different matter.

When Dane dumped me, it sent me into an awful tailspin. I felt worthless and stupid. People kept telling me that was just my depression talking, but the fact that my long-term boyfriend didn't want to be with me felt like proof that all the negative things I'd been thinking were correct.

Anyway, it's fine now. It really is. But I won't let it happen again.

I'll enjoy my remaining days with Julian, and then we'll go our separate ways.

Julian texts me in the afternoon, after a meeting about the Charles Fong Cardiology Wing. He told me about this earlier; it's the only meeting he's attending during his two weeks off.

He asks me to meet him at an Italian restaurant for dinner when I'm finished work, and he also asks if it's okay if he invites his brothers. Cedric is back in town and Julian wants to catch up, but he says he understands if I don't want to, if I'd prefer to see my sister after work or just spend time alone with him.

I'm curious to meet his other brother, and I decide I'm well enough to go.

When I step into the restaurant in Little Italy, Julian comes over and greets me with a kiss on the cheek. That relatively chaste kiss sends tingles all through my body.

Julian Fong is, indeed, a very powerful man.

We walk to the table, and he introduces me to Cedric.

Although Vince and Julian don't look much alike, I can see the resemblance between Julian and Cedric. They have similar builds and smiles, but Cedric's doesn't light me up the way Julian's does.

"So you're the woman who's got my brother buying phallic cacti and sunbathing in the middle of the week," Cedric says.

Vince walks over and takes the seat across from mine. "Cacti? Has Julian bought another one?"

"No," I say, "but I'm thinking of making him a terrarium. I'll name each cactus in it."

"Are they all going to be named after characters from *Friends*?"

"Dear God," Julian mutters, putting his hand to his forehead and shaking his head. "Please don't."

Despite his words, I know he enjoys his brothers' ribbing.

"Hmm," I say. "I'll think about it. And I'll put a picture of the terrarium in the scrapbook. Julian, honey, you still have to book our private scrapbooking lessons."

"Can I come, too?" Vince asks.

"Don't you have better things to do with your time?" Julian says. "Posing in calendars? Attending orgies?"

"Let me check my schedule." Vince pulls out his phone and swipes his finger over the screen a few times. I don't think he's actually looking at anything. "I have some free time on Saturday morning."

"Will you even be awake on Saturday morning?"

"Good point, good point. Maybe Sunday? My hangover and the girls I pick up should be gone by noon."

"We're going to Montreal this weekend," Julian says, "and honestly, I was hoping everyone would forget about the scrapbooking. Why do you want to attend a scrapbooking lesson anyway?"

"Because I would take great joy in watching your reaction when someone asks you to stencil hearts and flowers. Not that I have any idea what scrapbooking involves. I'm just making shit up."

"Clearly," Julian mutters.

"You're planning a romantic weekend in Montreal?" Cedric asks. "This is serious."

I shift uncomfortably in my seat, and Julian opens his mouth, probably to protest that it's not serious. But even though that's true, I don't want to hear him say the words, so I quickly change the subject.

"I hear you're a writer," I say to Cedric.

Unfortunately, this seems to be the wrong thing to say.

"I *was* a writer," he grunts. "I don't what I am now."

A brief silence settles over the table.

"Come on, man," Vince says. "You'll figure it out soon. Now, how about we order a bottle of wine. What do you like, Courtney?"

"I always let Julian pick. I don't know much about wine, except that there's white and red."

Cedric turns to Julian. "It doesn't bother you to hear her talk about wine like this? You're usually rather serious about your wine."

"I bet Courtney has other skills that make up for it," Vince says.

"Vince," Julian growls.

"I wasn't talking about *those* skills. But her skill at picking out phallic houseplants is definitely impressive, and she's succeeded in keeping you away from the office. Priya says you haven't been in since that first day. I didn't think you had it in you."

"He made me a nice three-course meal yesterday." The words pop out of my mouth before I can think better of it. I don't want to talk about last night's dinner.

Vince and Cedric exchange a look.

There's a sinking feeling in the pit of my stomach. Shit. They know about my breakdown and my depression. Julian must have told them.

I cannot handle his family knowing about that. I feel too exposed as it is.

Before I can shoot Julian a dirty look, Cedric says, "It's hard for me to imagine him doing anything in the kitchen beyond making an espresso. He's certainly never cooked for a girlfriend in the past. Or maybe he did and we just didn't hear about it."

Okay, I was wrong about the reason for their reaction. I breathe out a sigh of relief.

"I'll save you the speculation," Julian says. "I've never cooked a fancy meal for anyone but Courtney."

"He even baked last week," Vince says. "He made lemon squares and cookies, and Po Po loved them."

Cedric laughs. "If I bat my eyelashes real pretty, will you make me lemon squares?"

"I can make you lemon squares," Julian says, "but, please, for the love of God, don't bat your eyelashes."

Cedric does it anyway, in an exaggerated fashion, and we all laugh.

"Make me a batch of lemon squares, too," Vince says. "Preferably some special lemon squares with weed."

"Are you going to eat them off your latest fling's stomach?" Julian asks, then shakes his head. "Why did I put that image in my head?"

The waitress comes over. Julian orders a bottle of Cabernet

Sauvignon, which I think is a red wine, but I'm not sure. She soon returns with the wine, which is indeed red.

After she pours us each a small glass, Julian raises his glass in a toast. He glances at Cedric, and I think he wants to say something about how it's nice to have his brother back in Toronto, but in the end, he keeps it simple. "Cheers."

We all try our wine, then Cedric turns to me. "What do you do for work?"

"Biomedical research."

He whistles. "Your girlfriends are always impressive, Julian."

"I'm not that impressive," I protest. "It's not like I run my own lab."

"You're impressive," Julian murmurs, quietly enough so that only I can hear, and it sets me aflutter.

We talked about my research the other day at breakfast, and he asked some surprisingly intelligent questions.

Well, I suppose it wasn't actually surprising. This is Julian, after all, and he's good at everything.

I look at his brothers. "Tell me about the women he's dated." This is probably a bad idea, but I can't help being curious.

"Hmm," Cedric says. "There were a couple of lawyers—yeah, Julian definitely had a thing for lawyers for a while. Then there was a doctor, an engineer…"

"This sounds like the beginning of a bad joke," I say.

"Challenge accepted," Vince says, resting his hands on the back of his head. "A lawyer, a doctor, and an engineer—"

Julian holds up a hand. "I don't need to hear this."

"Thank God. I can't remember the rest of that joke. The drugs and alcohol must have fried my brain." Vince is being sarcastic. I think.

"You know," Cedric says, "two years ago, we never could have gone out for dinner like this. Vince would have been working fourteen-hour days, Julian would have been working fourteen-hour days, and I would have been on my book tour." He raises his wine glass, and we all clink glasses. "To being lazy!"

"Amen," Vince says before downing half his glass.

"Do you ever miss it?" Cedric asks.

"Why would I? I have money and no demands on my time. It's the perfect life."

Julian looks skeptical but says nothing. Soon, conversation switches to the design of the cardiology wing at East Markham Hospital.

The waitress brings us bread and takes our orders. The bread is as good as the stuff Julian served me yesterday, and I eagerly take a second slice.

I feel fine now. It's nice to hang out with people after work, and I like Julian's family.

But then I remind myself that I'll probably never see them again. Julian's two weeks of freedom are almost over; my two weeks in his life are almost over. We probably won't have time to take those scrapbooking lessons or make a terrarium.

I pull out my phone. "Let me take a picture of the three of you for the scrapbook."

We take a few pictures and sip our wine. Our appetizers arrive, and they're delicious.

"You doing okay?" Julian whispers.

"Yes," I say. "I'm just fine."

Except I've realized how hard it'll be to walk away from Julian Fong. Earlier I assumed it wouldn't be a big problem, but now I know otherwise.

I met his family, and he met mine. I let him see me at my worst; I told him my secrets.

It won't be easy, but all good things must come to an end. I know that all too well.

Somehow, I'll just have to deal.

WHEN WE LAND in Montreal on Friday night, a limo is waiting for us. I ask the driver to take us to the restaurant where I've made reservations, then bring the suitcases to our hotel. Admittedly, it's a little tempting to go straight to the hotel so I can untie the bow on Courtney's blouse and slide off the rest of her clothes, but that can wait just a little longer.

I get to spend all weekend with her. I am a lucky, lucky man.

"I haven't been in a limo since prom!" she says. "Should we help ourselves to a drink? Or maybe we could have sex. That's a thing people do in limos, isn't it?"

Oh, dear God. It's impossible not to think about getting her naked. Right here.

I press the button to push up the divider.

She puts her hands to her mouth. "Oops. I forgot about that."

"It's okay," I murmur, and then I kiss her. I slip my hand under her shirt, and she moans as I tweak her nipple. Encouraged, I push down her shirt and bra and take her nipple into my mouth. When she rolls her hips against me, I can't help unbuttoning her pants and sliding my hand inside her panties, running my finger along her folds.

I've been in a limo many, many times before. I've made out with a woman in a limo before. But I've always been careful to stop it from going any further than that.

However, I don't have much self-control where Courtney is concerned, and honestly, why not have some fun in the back of a limo? The last two weeks have been all about doing things I wouldn't normally do. Like baking lemon squares and binge-watching TV shows.

"Please tell me you have a condom," Courtney says, the last word coming out on a gasp as I slide a finger inside her.

"Mm. I'm saving it for later. But that doesn't mean you won't get an orgasm."

I know her body, and I know I can get her off with just my fingers.

I slide a second finger inside her and thrust in and out as I look at the pleasure written all over her face. "You're so pretty when you're being touched."

She makes some incoherent noises.

God, she feels good, and it's tempting to take the condom out of my pocket, but I don't want to show up at the restaurant looking like we just had sex in the back of a limo. My cock can't help hardening as I touch her, but it'll just have to wait.

I raise my hand to my mouth and lick her moisture off my index finger, then my middle finger, before licking my thumb. I love her taste. I can't wait to bury my face between her legs later.

"Please." She bucks her hips.

I slide my hand back into her pants, my fingers thrusting inside her, my thumb gently circling her clit. Our lips tremble as we look at each other, our faces nearly touching, and then I close the space between us and kiss her mouth. I work my lips over hers, flick my tongue against hers, and I swallow her cries as she comes apart in my arms.

By the time we show up at the restaurant, we've put ourselves back together.

More or less.

~

"I'm going to have the confit du canard," Courtney says after studying the menu for a minute. "What about you?"

"The lamb shank. Escargots to start, if you'd like to share?"

"Sure. I haven't had them in ages."

I spent hours trying to find the best places to eat in Montreal. Tonight, we're at a French bistro, sitting by the window on the second floor. I couldn't help but be pleased when we were shown to our table and Courtney proclaimed it "lovely."

The waiter comes over, and I order our food and a glass of wine each.

"Your French is really good," Courtney says after he leaves. "Mine is crap. I stopped taking French in grade ten, and I've forgotten almost everything I learned."

I lean forward and place my hand on her knee under the table. "Would you like if I spoke French in the bedroom? Would that turn you on?"

She grabs her water glass, seeming a little flustered. "I think, um...to be honest, it would probably make me laugh."

Our wine arrives, and Courtney takes a sip and smiles. "It's good."

I love seeing her drink wine. She claims she knows nothing about it, but she always seems to appreciate it.

And her sigh when she closes her eyes and pops the first bite of confit du canard in her mouth... Oh, God.

"This is amazing." She cuts off a piece and puts it on my plate.

"It is," I say after I try it.

Although I've had confit du canard a number of times before, it's like I'm having it for the first time. That's a common occurrence with Courtney. I feel like I'm doing lots of things for the first time, realizing I never fully appreciated them before.

Watching her eat crème brûlée is even more erotic than watching her eat duck. The noises she makes are positively sinful.

"That's it," I say. "We're getting out of here."

We make out in the limo on the way to the hotel, but it's only a five-minute ride, so we don't get any further than that. I wait impatiently as we check in. The receptionist insists on telling us where to find all sorts of things I don't care about right now.

"Breakfast is included in your stay. The breakfast room is just through those doors. We have a buffet with—"

"Got it," I say.

Can't everyone tell that I just want to be alone with the beautiful woman on my arm?

"If you turn left and walk past the elevators, you'll find the pool. The hours are—"

"Thank you, but we won't be swimming."

"The rooftop patio is available for all our guests. To get to the rooftop patio—"

"We'll figure it out when we need to."

"The fitness center…"

Finally, we enter our suite on the top floor.

"It's so big!" Courtney exclaims.

Okay, that's enough.

"I hope you say that about something else in a few minutes," I growl, wrapping my arms around her from behind and carrying her to bed.

"I want to check out the washroom and see if we have a fancy shower. Ooh, and the little shampoo bottles. Do you think they have gold lids?"

I glare at her. She laughs, and then I cover her mouth with mine and start working on her clothes as I kiss her. I slip off her shoes and pants before I start on the buttons on her pink blouse. Soon, she's wearing nothing but a black bra and panties, both edged with lace.

"Beautiful," I murmur, and before I can continue disrobing her, she's unbuttoning my shirt and pushing down my pants.

Now I'm naked, and she's still wearing her underwear...and she has her hand circled around my cock.

She kneels beside me and licks the tip as her hand slides up and down. Then she wraps her lips around the head and slowly, ever so slowly, takes me all the way into her mouth.

I grip the sheets and groan.

Nobody can affect me like she does. Absolutely no one.

I can't let this finish too quickly. I sit up and remove the rest of her clothing. I recall how she shyly stepped into my room last week, wearing one of my shirts, and told me it had been years since she'd had sex but she wanted to do it with me.

She's not shy around me anymore.

I settle her back on the multitude of pillows and kiss my way down her body, being sure to pay attention to the underside of her jaw—she particularly likes that spot—and her breasts. And then my mouth is between her legs, and I give her a long lick.

She jerks underneath me.

I lift my head. "Good?"

"Julian..." She pushes my head back down.

I smile as I lick her and thrust my fingers inside her at the same time. She feels so good and, God, I need to be inside her heat; I need to have everything I can with her. I pull the condom out of my discarded pants and roll it on. I watch her face as I push inside, her pleasure as I fill her up.

Slowly, I begin to thrust, and I kiss every part of her I can reach. Her shoulders, her collarbone, her wrists. Everything about her is wonderful, and I can't get enough. She wraps her legs around my hips, taking me even deeper, and I groan. Then she rolls us over so I'm beneath her and, fuck, she looks hot on top of me, her hands going to her breasts so she can touch herself as she moves. My hands drift to her plump ass and give it a squeeze.

We take our time, slow and sensual movements of hips, skin against skin.

"You feel so amazing," she says, and I don't think any compliment has ever meant more to me. I want to always make her feel amazing.

I flip her over and increase my pace, leading us to the inevitable ending, our orgasms overtaking us at the same time.

~

After sex, we have a long shower together and Courtney finds great amusement in us wearing the fluffy white robes provided by the hotel.

"We match!" she says, and she insists we wear them until bedtime.

By midnight, she's asleep and I've got my head propped up on my elbow, looking at her lovely face in the shadows of the hotel room.

Old Julian would have considered this a terrible waste of time. If he couldn't fall asleep in thirty minutes, he would get up and do some work.

But now I'm simply staring at the sleeping woman who has turned my life upside down in the past two weeks. We only have two more days together. Earlier, I tried to push that thought to the back of my mind and focus on having a good time with Courtney, but now, in the dark stillness of the night, I can't help but think of the end.

When we get back from Montreal, we'll go to my condo, and she'll pack up her stuff while I write her a check for five thousand dollars. Then she'll walk out of my life, having fulfilled her job of teaching me how to have fun. She's certainly made my break from work more fun than I thought it would be, that's for sure.

I can't lie to myself. I don't want this to end.

It doesn't have to, does it? I could ask her to stay.

But after Olivia, I swore off relationships because I was so terrible at them. I don't want to be like Vince, always with a different girl. Frankly, that sounds exhausting. I'd prefer to be committed to one woman, to go home to someone I care about after a day's work. A string of flings cannot compare to that. This isn't something I've just discovered about myself; I've always felt this way.

Except that when I get home from the office, it's usually eight or nine o'clock at night, and I still need to send a few emails. We'd hardly have any time together.

Part of me is itching to do some work again and feel productive. I can't bake lemon squares and sun tan on the patio forever, though I definitely needed that break. As much as I hate to admit it, my family was right about something. But when I return to work, I won't have Courtney anymore. I can't put it off any longer—it's my company, and I need to run it—and like it or not, she's just not compatible with my regular life.

I sigh and turn onto my other side so I can't see her anymore, but I can still hear her breathe and feel her warm presence beside me.

I'll remember this as long as I live.

"I've always wanted to order room service," Courtney says when we wake up on Saturday, "but it was too expensive to justify. Maybe we can do it this morning?" She gets on her knees and presses her hands together. "Please? I'll give you sexual favors."

"You'd give me sexual favors anyway," I say.

"True."

Unfortunately, room service arrives faster than expected. There's enough time for her to get me off, but not enough time for me to make her scream. When I hear a knock on the door, I have my mouth between her legs.

"Shit," I mutter, scrambling up and pulling on a robe. She giggles as she pulls on hers.

Once we're decent, I open the door and a little cart is rolled into our room. There's a pot of coffee, orange juice, and two domes to keep our plates warm. We eat breakfast together, as we've done many times before. I remember the first breakfast I made for her. Eggs and bacon, like we're having now.

After today, there will be only one more breakfast.

"Are you okay?" she asks.

Shit. I didn't realize my displeasure was showing on my face.

"Just fine," I say. "I can't wait to spend the day with you."

"Me, too."

We smile at each other, but my smile is a little forced.

After a leisurely breakfast—and me finishing what I'd started before our food arrived—we head out and walk around Old Montreal. I take Courtney's hand in mine, and she doesn't let go, except to point at things that interest her.

For today, I can pretend I have a girlfriend. I will do my best to forget reality.

Courtney is admiring some art in the window of a gallery when I look at my watch.

"Crap," I say. "We've only got five minutes."

"Five minutes until what?"

"You'll see."

We hurry down the narrow sidewalks until we reach a tiny pâtisserie. There's a line-up outside, but I made reservations, so we bypass the line. Courtney and I are seated at a table in the back and given pastry menus. Everything sounds tasty.

"Let's get a chocolate éclair," she says. "Wait…no. The strawberry éclair."

"I thought you'd want the chocolate-raspberry tart."

After all the meals we've eaten together in the past couple of weeks, I've gotten a pretty good idea of what Courtney likes. She's particularly fond of raspberry-flavored things.

"Yes!" she exclaims. "How did I miss that before?"

"I think we should get the chocolate cake with salted caramel, too."

"Hmm..."

The waitress comes around and asks if we're ready to order.

Ha. Not even close.

Courtney frowns at the menu. "I bet the croissants are good here. Maybe we should get a croissant. Except you can get a croissant anywhere... Sorry for being so slow at this. I'll get the chocolate-raspberry tart, and you can get the chocolate cake with salted caramel, and I promise not to steal more than half."

"Why don't we get three things to share?"

We choose a strawberry éclair for our third pastry, and we also order a pot of tea. When our food arrives, she takes a few pictures—for our scrapbook, she says—before trying a bite of the tart.

"This is the greatest thing ever." She moans in pleasure.

After tomorrow, I won't get to hear that sound again. My chest constricts.

"Well, it's the greatest thing ever except for...you know." She does something weird with her left eye.

"Were you trying to wink?"

"Obviously." She does it again. It's adorable, but it looks more like she has a bug in her eye than a sexy wink.

"I hate to tell you this," I say, "but you're very bad at winking. Have you ever looked in the mirror while doing it?"

"No, but I'm going to right now."

Before I can protest and say it can wait, she's gotten up from her chair and started toward the washroom. I resist the urge to finish all the pastries in her absence.

She comes back with a sober look on her face. "You're right. I can't wink. I tried with my right eye, too, and it was even worse."

"Let me see."

"No way. It's embarrassing."

"If you show me, you can have the rest of the chocolate-raspberry tart."

Apparently, this is enough of an incentive, and Courtney does something funny with her right eye, then bursts into laughter.

"It's awful, isn't it?" she asks between laughs.

"Yeah, it kind of is." Since she's laughing, I can't help but laugh, too.

This is something Old Julian never would have done: just sitting in a pâtisserie with a woman, eating dessert and drinking tea and laughing together. Before Courtney, I never would have taken a spontaneous trip to Montreal, and I would have checked my phone at least twice since we sat down. I wouldn't have been able to lose myself in the moment.

That's when it hits me.

I'm different from who I was before, so maybe I *can* have a relationship.

When I first decided to go along with my family's plan, I thought I'd have a break, then be refreshed when I went back to my life of non-stop work. I didn't expect the time off to actually change me.

But I don't want to work fourteen-hour days anymore. Although a part of me is eager to get back to the office, I hate the idea of doing nothing but work now. Sure, I'd like Fong Investments to grow and become even more of a success, but not at the expense of me having no life whatsoever. I want to have time to read on my rooftop patio, wander around the city, eat pistachio gelato...

And I want Courtney to be with me.

I wonder if this was part of my family's plan when they ordered me to take two weeks off work. Maybe they thought it would not only give me a break but make me realize I need a better work-life balance. Work-life balance isn't something I thought about before—I was too busy working to think about it. And if my workaholic tendencies put a serious strain on a relationship, that's a serious problem and I should seek professional help rather than just resigning myself to never having a significant other.

Unlike my past relationships, I'm emotionally invested in this. I haven't been holding myself back with Courtney. Is it because I haven't had to worry about work in the past two weeks, or is it because of her?

I think it's because of her. She's special. I feel a sense of peace and enjoyment with her that I've never felt with another girlfriend; I feel like I'm more than a workaholic CEO in her presence, more than the responsible son who gets things done.

The idea that I could really be with Courtney still feels new and fragile and hard to believe, but it might be possible after all.

Full of pastries, we begin walking up Mont Royal, the small mountain within the city. It's a lovely late-summer day, the blue sky dotted with fluffy white clouds. When we get to the top, Courtney takes lots of pictures, once again saying it's for our scrapbook. Then we hike along a trail through the woods. At one point, I pull her to the side of the trail, wrap my arms around her from behind, and kiss my way up her neck. At first she laughs, and then she sighs…and then my lips meet hers. We're trying to get closer, closer, closer…

By the time we reach the large cross at the other end of the mountaintop, gray clouds are rolling in. The image of the cross against the darkening sky seems ominous, and I shiver despite the warm air.

It feels like something bad is going to happen.

But what? I'm on vacation with a pretty girl, and it's going well.

I push that odd feeling aside.

As we descend the mountain, it starts to sprinkle. We walk

faster in the hopes of reaching the hotel before it pours, but the rain quickly becomes heavier. I didn't even think to check the weather earlier. It looked like such a nice day.

There's a crack of thunder in the distance. Courtney starts running, laughing as though it was her plan to get caught in the rain all along. I easily match her stride, and soon we're running together through the rain, getting absolutely soaked, but it's okay.

It's fine. It's great.

The weather is still warm, so I'm not cold, even though my clothes are drenched. Courtney's T-shirt clings attractively to her chest.

Suddenly, I realize she isn't beside me anymore, and I stop and turn back. She's several paces behind me, bent over with her hands on her legs.

"Sorry," she says as I approach. "I'm not in the greatest shape."

When she straightens up, she slides her fingers through my wet hair and kisses me. Her mouth is warmer and sweeter than the rain and I don't want to let go. Ever.

I love her.

The feeling consumes me. I love Courtney, and it feels different from every time this has happened to me before.

I have no choice: I *need* to make this work.

I pull back and look into her eyes.

"Julian?"

Even though I know what I want, what I *need*, I can't get the words out.

I've had many tough phone calls and business meetings, but none of them caused the anxiety that revealing my feelings to Courtney does.

When we were at Chris's Coffee Shop, she told me she wasn't interested in a relationship. Then again, she also told me she wasn't interested in a casual fling, and look what happened.

But there was nothing casual about it from the start, was there? I asked her to move in with me—temporarily, but still—

within a few minutes of learning her name. That's not like me; I'm usually more cautious. Everything has been different with her, and it feels like some part of me knew she was special from the very beginning.

She told me about her struggles with mental illness, but I'm not afraid of her depression. I want her no matter what, and I'll find a way to solve her problems.

No, my fear is that she'll turn me down. After all, she said she didn't do relationships. I have reason to think she shares my feelings, but I can't be certain, and if she turns me down now, it would ruin what we have left of the weekend. I don't want to do that.

I can't bring myself to tell her yet. I'll wait just a little longer.

"Julian?" she says again.

"It's nothing. Nothing at all."

And I kiss her once more.

It stops raining when we arrive at the hotel, the storm perfectly timed for us to get soaked. When we get back to our room, we spend an hour sitting in bed in our white bathrobes, wet clothes in a pile on the floor and cups of tea in our hands. Then Courtney goes to the washroom to get ready for dinner, saying she wants her outfit to be a surprise. I haven't seen the dress she bought with Naomi, nor have I seen her new shoes.

I put on a gray suit and sit on the bed. I tap my foot on the carpeted floor as I wait for her. We're not late. It's only five and our reservation isn't until seven, though we plan to have a drink at a cocktail bar first. But I'm impatient to see her all dressed up.

I pick up my phone and pull up a stupid game. I play a few rounds before the door clicks open and Courtney emerges from the washroom.

She's wearing a black dress that clings to her chest almost as much as the wet T-shirt, and the skirt flares out and ends just below her knees. It's stunning. It's like the dress was made just for her, to enhance all of her features. She's radiant and sexy as hell, and I do not want to wait until the end of the evening to be inside her.

"New plan," I say, my voice rough. "We'll have the cocktails after dinner. But now..." I reach for the zipper at the side of the dress and press myself against her back.

"I just put this on. You can't take it off already."

"Watch me."

She laughs. "No. It took me a long time to get dressed up for tonight. I won't let you undo it all before we leave the hotel room."

"Fine," I grumble. "If you insist."

She walks toward the door, swaying her hips and driving me crazy.

Today has been almost like a dream, with room service and picture-perfect pastries and kissing in the rain.

But I know it won't all be like this. I know a relationship is more than sex and fancy dinners and jetting off to Montreal, and I want all of it with her. I want to be there when she's down, I want to be there when homemade apple crumble and vanilla ice cream taste like ash in her mouth—it will pain me to see her like that, but I want to be there, and I want to help her.

I care for her so very much.

"Julian," she says, once I've been quiet for a minute, "are you *still* ogling my ass?"

I'D WANTED to tease Julian and make him think about sex all evening, but I hadn't realized it would do the same to me. Now I wish I'd agreed to skip cocktails and let him screw me before we left the hotel.

Not that my cocktail wasn't delicious. It had cherry and black pepper and vodka and some kind of herb and…hell, I don't know. All I know is that it tasted marvelous.

But we've been at the restaurant for almost two hours now. Dinner shows no sign of ending anytime soon, and he's looking so damn gorgeous.

I've always liked men in suits, and nobody wears a suit like Julian. It hints at large muscles underneath, and I want to grab those muscles and scrape my fingernails over them and lick them, just generally have my way with him.

We're at a special restaurant that only has a tasting menu. When I saw the price, I nearly had a heart attack, but then I plastered on a smile and said, "Sure, sounds good," as though eating at fancy restaurants was just a regular occurrence for me. For the past two weeks, I suppose it has been, though none of the restaurants we went to in Toronto were quite like *this*.

The food is delicious. I'm not sure what everything is, and the menu was full of words like "emulsion" and "deconstructed" and "foam," but it's all wonderful. The servings are small, however, and there are lots of courses to form a complete meal. I'm not quite full, but at this point I would be content to go back to the hotel, have sex, and order room service at midnight.

The other problem is that because we're at a nice restaurant and not alone in our room, I can't lick the plates clean. I have to remember my manners. Whereas back at the hotel...

Well, I'd be able to use my tongue as much as I like.

When our second dessert arrives forty-five minutes later, I nearly shriek with delight before I've even tasted it. After this, we're done!

"Excited about something?" Julian murmurs, sliding his hand under the hem of my dress and up my knee.

I try not to squirm as I shake my head.

"Hmm." He picks up his dessert fork, then puts it down and rests his chin on his hand. "There's another cocktail bar that sounds quite good. What do you say we go there and have another drink before—"

"No!" I say.

Then I realize he was joking.

He gives me a slow smile, and his gaze travels down my face, my neck, and comes to rest on my cleavage. There's no way he wants to have another drink before he gets under my dress.

Though I suppose going back to the hotel isn't strictly necessary. I glance down the hall. There are two individual bathrooms, which are small but sufficient for...

My cheeks burn.

I was actually considering having sex in the bathroom of one of the most expensive restaurants in Montreal.

I look down at my dessert. I have no idea what it is, but the plating is a work of art, and when I have a bite, chocolate and fruit explode in my mouth. It's so creamy and rich and, God, I'm glad we didn't leave early. Perhaps the dessert is even good enough to give me an orgasm.

But it would be nowhere near as good as what Julian can do to me.

As soon as he's paid the bill, I jump up from the table and stumble on my new heels. Luckily, Julian is there to catch me so I don't make too much of a scene.

We walk back to the hotel—less than ten minutes—in silence, but my entire body is aware of him. I'm impatient as we wait for the elevator, hopping from one foot to the other. Finally, it comes, and we take it to the top floor. Once Julian steps off, he starts walking slowly with an exaggerated swagger.

"Julian!" I squeak. "Stop it."

Although I'm annoyed because I want him to hurry to the room and have sex with me, I'm also amused. When I first met Julian, I wouldn't have imagined him being playful like this.

But once we get to the room, he's all business. He presses me against the door, pins my hands over my head, and takes my mouth in his. His kiss is wild, desperate.

"I can't believe you made me wait all night," he says.

He's already sliding up my skirt and pushing aside my panties. His finger plunges inside me, and I squirm against him. He's still holding my arms above my head with his other hand.

"I can't believe it either," I say on a gasp. "It was a mistake."

"An awful, awful mistake. Don't you worry, we'll make up for it now."

His mouth is on mine again, his fingers between my legs. I am so wet for him, and I want *more*. I want to feel him inside me; I want to be full of him. I want all I can get.

He tilts his head away from me. His lips are parted, eyes dark and focused intently on mine. This face has become so dear to me in the past two weeks, but our time together is almost over.

I banish that thought from my mind.

"I can't wait any longer," he says.

I breathe heavily. "Neither can I."

He spins me around so I'm facing the door and presses the length of his body against mine. His erection is hard against my lower back, and oh God, I want him even more now. Then he's gone and I miss his heat, but my skin prickles as I realize he's opening his pants. He can't wait until we get to bed. He's going to fuck me right here, against the door, both of us fully clothed.

He rolls on a condom before shoving aside my panties again and rubbing the tip of his cock against me.

"Yes," I moan, pressing back against him. "Yes."

He pushes inside, and I start shaking. He's in me, and it feels so right and good.

His thrusts are fast and deep. It's nothing like the first time, when we were wrapped up in bed together and he was so tender with me. This time, it's rough and needy, but that's exactly what I want right now. So many different things are perfect with him.

I clutch the door handle, needing to anchor myself. Julian is fucking me harder, grabbing my ass, filling me with such intense sensation—I never knew it could be like this. My orgasm builds, and when it crashes over me, I hardly know what's happening. I think I might be falling, but I know he's got me.

He growls and shakes as he finishes inside me. When he pulls out, he wraps his arms around me, and we slide to the floor together and don't say anything for a long time.

Eventually, he pulls me to my feet.

"Let's go to bed," he says.

We have sex again in bed. This time, we're naked and our touches are less frantic. Instead, it's slow and romantic.

Afterward, he falls sleep, the lamp beside the bed still on, and I prop my head up on my hand and look down at him.

We've had our fling, and he's been a wonderful lover. He's

wonderful in every way, in fact. But on Monday, I'll go back to my regular life. No more penthouses and expensive hotels and tasting menus.

That's okay. I don't need luxury; I like my ordinary little apartment.

But I'll miss seeing Julian Fong every day. I'll miss him so much.

I let out a choked little cry.

I'm screwed.

I told myself I could handle the end, but now, I don't think I can, and if I'm honest with myself, I was aware of that all along. I knew Julian would get to me, but I wanted him so badly that I was able to lie to myself so I could have what I craved.

Or maybe it would have been like this even if I hadn't slept with him. We were still living together, spending so much time together.

I am so, so screwed.

My heart lurches in my chest. It wasn't supposed to get involved, but it did.

This is the last thing I need, especially when I can feel the impending doom of depression coming my way. Dealing with heartbreak on top of that…well, last time it almost killed me.

That's not an exaggeration. I was in the hospital on suicide watch. I couldn't take care of myself; I could barely even breathe. I just wished everything would end, wished I could crawl into a dark cave and disappear from my own life.

This won't technically be a breakup, because Julian and I were never officially in a relationship, but it's heartbreak nonetheless. He'll go back to his regular life, and I'll go back to mine.

I cry silent tears into the night.

The next morning is our last in Montreal. We wake up around

eight, both still naked after last night's activities, and we simply hold each other. I try to enjoy this while it lasts, but maybe I should start extricating myself. Maybe it'll be less painful if I start putting some distance between us now.

I start to slither out of Julian's embrace, but he holds me still.

"I have something to ask you," he says.

"Okay." He'll ask me his question, and then I'll get up and have my shower.

But when I look into his eyes, I can tell it's something big.

"I don't want this to end," he says.

Neither do I! Neither do I!

"I like you a lot, Courtney. When I first came up to you in the coffee shop, you were savoring your gingerbread latte..." He scrubs a hand over his face, and I realize he's nervous. It's not like him, and it melts my heart, which is bouncing around in my chest like mad. "I wanted to pay you five thousand dollars to teach me to enjoy life, and I suggested we could have a fling, too." He chuckles. "It sounds crazy, doesn't it? But now that I've gotten to know you, I want more than a fling."

I can't contain my goofy smile.

"I told you I didn't do relationships anymore," he says. "I suck at them because I'm at the office all the time. However, you make me want to try again, and after the last two weeks, I think I've changed. I'll be less of a workaholic come Monday morning, and I'll spend as much time with you as I can."

It's everything I could ask for.

"Yes," I say. "I don't want this to end, either."

He grins. "I'll still give you the money, of course. What are you going to do with it?"

"Give it to Naomi. It was perfect timing, actually. She'd just told me she couldn't afford the trip to New York we'd planned, and later that day, you showed up and offered me your ridiculous deal. So now we can go on the trip, and she can have a little extra money...and I can have you."

Julian proceeds to kiss me very, very thoroughly, then offers to solve any financial problems I might have in the future.

～

I should be happy, but when we're on the plane back to Toronto, I feel a prickle of doubt.

My depression is returning. Every five years.

It's hard to imagine that my life will get so terrible so soon, when things have been pretty good recently, aside from the occasional meltdown. But my depression is inevitable, like the changing seasons. Even Julian, as powerful as he is, won't be able to stop it, and I can't imagine he'll want to be with me when he sees what it's really like. I won't be Fun Courtney who squeals in delight over fancy pastries. I assume a lot of the reason he likes me is because of the joy I take in the world around me, but when I'm depressed, that becomes impossible. Sure, he was lovely to me when I had my "depression attack" a few days ago, but once that becomes a constant state for me, it'll be different.

Dane couldn't handle it, and we'd already been together for a while at that point. I can't imagine Julian will enjoy it when his new girlfriend becomes a dark cloud of messed-up thoughts who can barely make it out of bed—and not because she wants to have sex all the time.

That's another thing. Depression kills my libido.

I feel more than a prickle of doubt now; I'm being smacked in the face with it.

How can this possibly work?

I'll go out with him for a little while, and then he'll dump me and break my heart, and it will be just like ten years ago. I'll have to go on leave from my job and I'll stop sleeping and I'll be such a bother to Naomi but she'll do it because she loves me, and…

Julian places a hand on my shoulder. "Are you okay? You've been reading the same page for ten minutes."

"I'm fine."

I must not sound very convincing.

"What is it?" he asks, rubbing circles on my shoulder with his thumb.

He's a sweet man. You wouldn't think the CEO of an investment company would be sweet, but he is.

I swallow. "My depression. I told you how I have a severe episode every five years, right? It'll start soon. It always starts in the fall. I'll become difficult to be around, and you won't want to be with me anymore. Like my ex."

"Not true. I'll want to be with you no matter what. I care for you, and I will be there."

He says it with such conviction. I offer him a small smile, but I'm not convinced. I'm not the sort of girlfriend a man like Julian should have. He needs someone who's less of a mess. Someone who will look stunning on his arm at charity galas and always know the right thing to say.

Even if I'm able to have a boyfriend, he's probably not the type of boyfriend I should have, either. He's always busy. He says he's different now, but maybe that just means he'll work thirteen-hour days instead of fourteen. Could he really be supportive when he's working his ass off?

I have doubts. I have so many doubts. But I shove them aside.

Because I want, more than anything, to be with Julian, and I'm feeling a bit delusional at the moment. I feel like believing when I shouldn't believe.

He's become an important part of my life; he means so much to me now. Being without him is too painful to contemplate. I don't have a choice.

I might be on a sinking ship, but there's nowhere else for me to go.

[24]
JULIAN

I walk into work nice and early on Monday morning. Fortunately, the lock on my office door hasn't been changed, as Po Po threatened to do, and I'm at my desk by seven.

It feels good to be back. I'm itching to get some work done and make sure everything hasn't gone to shit in my absence. I don't think it has, but doubtless there will be fires to put out.

However, I've only answered one email when Vince swaggers into my office.

"Just checking that you made it back to the office after your holiday," he says.

"I'm here and I'm working. Or, rather, I would be working if you hadn't interrupted."

"That's what I do best."

"It is, though I'm surprised you're awake at seven fifteen in the morning."

He shrugs. "Haven't gone to bed yet."

I look at my brother, really look at him for once. His clothes are loose, and there are dark circles under his eyes, and his cocky smile is a little strained.

I get up from my desk and walk over to him. "Are you okay?"

"Why wouldn't I be okay? I've been up all night doing hookers and drugs. I just need a few hours of sleep, that's all."

There are some brown stains at the bottom of his T-shirt. I won't ask.

But I'll ask about something else.

"Do you have a drug problem? Should I be concerned?"

With Vince, I no longer know what's real and what's a joke. I know he parties, and he always seems to have a different woman —based on his Facebook pictures—but a lot of the things he says have to be an exaggeration.

Or are they? I couldn't say.

And then there's the way he keeps showing up at my condo and office, as though he's desperate for company.

Vince rolls his eyes. "I smoke pot on occasion. You gonna tell Mom? You gonna make me to go to rehab?"

"I'm sure there's nothing wrong with the occasional joint. Just don't hotbox my office."

"Thanks for the great idea. I'm surprised you know what hotboxing is, to be honest."

Okay, this conversation has gotten off-track.

I take a deep breath. "Something isn't right with you, and I want to know what it is."

"Why?" Vince folds his arms over his chest.

I frown. "Because you're my brother and I…care about you."

It's hard to say those words to Vince. This is not the kind of relationship we have. But it's suddenly obvious that although I think of him as a partying playboy, it's far from the whole truth.

He lets out a bark of laughter. "Your girlfriend's turned you into Mr. Touchy-Feely."

Well, I certainly do a lot of *touching* with her, that's for sure.

"Just to clarify, she actually *is* my girlfriend now." I smile. I can't help it.

"I look forward to seeing a scrapbook of the first month of your relationship."

"Back to you. Are you—"

"Julian!" Priya barges into my office, carrying a double espresso. "How was your vacation?"

"You didn't need to come in at seven thirty," I say, annoyed at the interruption.

"It's your first day back. Don't worry, I won't be here until eight tomorrow. You have my word." She hands me the espresso.

"His vacation was great," Vince says, apparently deciding I'm incapable of answering. He's probably relieved our conversation was cut short. "He got himself a girlfriend."

"Really?" Priya says. "That's fantastic. What's her name?"

"Courtney," Vince replies before I can say anything. "She bought him a cactus shaped like a penis!"

I put my head in my heads. "Dear God. Why do you need to be like this?"

"Is it true?" Priya asks. "About the cactus?"

"Well, I paid for the cactus, but she told me to do it. It's true that Joey is rather phallic-shaped, although..." I trail off as I realize my mistake.

Priya tilts her head. "Joey? The cactus has a name?"

Vince claps me on the back. "Good going, dude." He turns to Priya. "They're going to take scrapbooking lessons together! I wonder what else. Maybe salsa classes?"

"Look," I say, "I haven't been at work in more than two weeks, and I have a lot to do. Could you please go somewhere else to discuss my love life?"

Just then, my father walks into the room. "I heard about this love life of yours. Your mother seems quite taken with your new woman, although apparently you claim she isn't really your girlfriend."

"You haven't heard the news," Vince says. "They're officially going out now. Oh, this is so exciting!" He squeals like a preteen girl at a Justin Bieber concert.

"Vince." Dad gives him a look. "What's wrong with you? Are you on drugs?"

"Nothing more than the occasional joint," he says cheerfully.

Vince and I need to have a proper conversation later when I'm not at work, though it's practically impossible to have a proper conversation with him these days.

"Right," Dad says. "Of course."

My father is a very successful businessman, with a presence to match, but he's actually rather soft-spoken. Yet when he talks, people listen.

Except for me and my brothers. We rarely listened when we were young, but now, I value my father's opinion, and he needs to get me up to speed on what's happened in the past two weeks.

"Alright," I say. "Vince, Priya, party's over. Vince, go home and sleep."

"Yes, Mom."

I gesture to the door. "Out. We have work to do."

They finally retreat.

I sit down behind my desk, and Dad takes the seat across from me.

"How do you like being back in the office?" I ask him.

"It's a nice change. Playing golf every day gets boring after a while." He pauses. "How was your vacation, aside from the getting-a-girlfriend part?"

I can't separate Courtney from my vacation. She was an important part of it.

But I haven't had a headache in more than a week, I've been sleeping better, and I'm not nearly as tense. I feel well-rested and re-energized. Ready to take on the world.

"I hate to admit I was wrong," I say, "but I was. I did need a holiday. And I also learned a thing or two about work-life balance."

Dad chuckles. "It's important. Now, when am I going to meet your new girlfriend?"

"Soon," I promise.

I don't see Courtney on Monday or Tuesday. She wants to spend a few nights in her apartment, and I'm working my usual days—thirteen hours or more. I tell myself I won't keep this up and it's just because I've been away for more than two weeks. Plus, our text messages provide a nice distraction.

On Wednesday, I leave work at six thirty, and she comes to my place for dinner. Takeout this time, rather than a three-course meal I cooked from scratch. She smiles and talks about her day, telling me briefly about her experiments and the antics of her friend Bethany's toddler.

Still, I have this feeling, like when we were on Mont Royal and the sky darkened, that something bad is coming. Except when we were in Montreal, nothing bad ended up happening. It rained, we kissed, and I realized I love her. That's all.

Nothing bad will happen now, either. I asked her to be with me, and she said yes. Life is good.

I haven't told Courtney I love her. I think it's a little early to say it out loud, so I settle for sending her long strings of heart emojis instead.

But I'll tell her soon.

I DON'T SEE Julian on Thursday or Friday, since he's slammed with work. He goes to work on Saturday, too, but I meet him at a restaurant in Chinatown for dinner—Chinatown on Spadina, not Chinatown East near where I live. Afterward, he shows me where his grandparents' bakery on Elizabeth Street used to be, in what is now Nathan Phillips Square. In the northwest corner of the square are two plaques about Toronto's original Chinatown.

I feel silly for not having known about this, but my family didn't immigrate here until the eighties. Most of my school friends' families came over around the same time, before the Chinese takeover of Hong Kong. But there were Chinese people in Toronto long before that.

"You know what I'm craving?" I say. "A pineapple bun. Let's buy some on the way back to your place."

"Actually..." He looks down at the plaques. "I have to go back to the office for an hour."

"You were already there for ten hours. And it's Saturday."

"I know. I'm sorry, but I didn't get to finish everything before our dinner date. You go back to my place, and I'll meet you there soon."

"Okay," I say, feeling a bit deflated.

When he arrives home from work, it's nine o'clock, and we watch a movie before going to bed. Sunday, he doesn't work at all, aside from sending a few emails in the morning, and we spend the day together.

It's good. I can't complain.

～

Once again, I don't see Julian on Monday or Tuesday, but on Wednesday, I decide to take an extra-long lunch break and surprise him at work. I stop in Chinatown to buy soup dumplings and pineapple buns, then head up to his office.

I've never been here before. The office is buzzing with activity, lots of people in suits rushing around.

"I'm here to see Julian Fong," I tell the receptionist.

She raises an eyebrow. "Do you have an appointment?"

"Um, no." I pause. "I'm his girlfriend."

"I see," she says, as though she doesn't see at all and thinks I'm full of shit. "I'll call his assistant. What's your name?"

"Courtney," I squeak.

The receptionist leads me to Julian's assistant, Priya, who gives me a much warmer greeting.

"I've heard so much about you," she says.

"You have?" What on earth has Julian been telling her?

"Not really. But I know of your existence, which is saying something."

"I brought him lunch." I hold up the white plastic bag with my purchases.

Her face falls. "I'm sorry. He's in a lunch meeting."

Right. People like Julian Fong have things like lunch meetings. He doesn't need me to bring him food.

I look at the bag, then turn back to Priya. "Want some soup dumplings?"

One of the delicate dumplings broke on my trip to Fong Investments, but otherwise, they're good. Priya has never had soup dumplings before, but she likes them. We split a pineapple bun, and I save the other for Julian. At first, I'm a little jealous of this young, attractive woman who works with Julian all day. However, it soon becomes clear that although she's fond of him, it's not like *that*. In fact, it sounds like she thinks of him as an older brother, and when she mentions her boyfriend, the last prickle of doubt I had is erased.

"Next time," she says, "you should call me first, and I'll let you know if he's available."

Julian strides in a little after one o'clock. He stops when he sees me by Priya's desk.

"Courtney?" he says, like he's not sure it's actually me, like he's confused to see me in this part of his life.

I jump up. "I, um, brought you lunch, but Priya told me you had a lunch meeting, so we shared the soup dumplings, and... here." I thrust a paper bag toward him. "Here's your pineapple bun."

My boyfriend is wearing a pinstripe suit, and I'm wearing the casual clothes I usually wear to the lab. He smiles at me. "I think I have three minutes until my next meeting."

I can't help feeling disappointed. I came all this way to see him, waited half an hour, gave away his dumplings, and now he only has three minutes for me.

But really, it's my fault for not calling first.

He ushers me into his office, and as soon as he closes the door, his mouth is on mine.

Yes, that's better.

He pulls back and tucks a lock of hair behind my ear. "You taste like pineapple bun. Not that I'm complaining."

I look around his office. It's large and the furniture and art on the walls look quite expensive.

I don't belong here.

I put my arms around him because at least I feel like I belong when I'm holding him.

"Sorry I don't have more time," he says. "Is everything okay?"

"It's fine. I just thought I'd surprise you at work."

"I appreciate it."

"I have a present for you." I pull out a flash drive. "I won't tell you what's on it. You'll have to look for yourself once I've left."

He nods as he slides it into his pocket. "I can't wait until I have you alone tomorrow." He winks at me before I leave.

I'm very much looking forward to tomorrow.

That evening, I do a stupid thing.

I Google my boyfriend.

Among the news about Fong Investments and his family's philanthropy, I find a picture of Julian and a beautiful woman at a gala. According to the caption, her name is Olivia Tremblay. She's wearing a stunning blue gown and she has a perfectly-messy updo. She's smiling up at Julian, who is turned partially away from the camera, with adoring eyes. Another Google search reveals she's a lawyer at a prestigious firm. Julian mentioned an ex named Olivia once, so I know they were actually together.

But they're not together anymore. He's with me and he cares for me, and sometimes he's in such a rush to be inside me that he doesn't wait until we're in the bedroom. It might be hard to believe, but this man wants me. He's the one who suggested we have something more. When I mentioned my depression, he said he'd be there for me, and he's seen me when I'm in a bad place.

If Julian were here right now and I spilled out all my insecurities, he would tell me again that he wants me. If I told Naomi, she would reassure me, too.

Although it's not cold, I wrap myself in a fuzzy blanket and sit down on my recliner with a cup of tea, a few gingersnaps, and one of my favorite novels. This is what I do when I start to feel shitty: I try to treat myself well. Sometimes I also do little things that make me feel productive, like putting away the dishes or throwing the garbage down the chute.

I've only read a few pages when my mind starts to wander.

Julian should have a more fashionable girlfriend who's less of a mess—like I was thinking on the plane. He shouldn't be with someone who struggled to finish her degree.

No, it's silly of me to think like that. Besides, I'm hardly an intellectual slouch—I have a PhD, for God's sake—and I had to take a break from school because I was sick. That's nothing to be ashamed of.

I pick up a gingersnap and dip it in the tea. I nibble the softened part of the cookie, then bite into the harder part.

It's sweet and a little spicy...and yet I can't really taste it. I can't enjoy it.

I force myself to return to the book in my lap. I read a page, then realize I have no idea what I just read, so I read it again, and I sort of, kind of, understand.

This is embarrassing. I can't even understand a goddamn chick lit novel that I've read several times before. Who the fuck gave me a PhD?

Well, at least it's not a PhD in English literature.

I struggle to keep reading, now going at an extremely slow pace, and I keep drinking my tea. I'm getting a tiny bit calmer, but not much.

I toss the book on the floor. What's the fucking point? I'm coming up to my regularly-scheduled episode of depression, and nothing can help me when I'm in the middle of that.

But then I remind myself that even if the fuzzy blanket, tea, and book don't make me feel good, sometimes they make me feel a little less bad, even when I'm in the throes of severe depression. There's still reason to do self-care even when I continue to feel shitty.

Ugh. Why does Julian's ex have to be so damn beautiful?

I need to forget about Olivia Tremblay. That was the past.

Still, I find myself Googling her again, and from a quick look at her Facebook account, I discover she's now married.

She doesn't matter. She's moved on. Julian's moved on.

Why can't I understand a fucking chick lit book?

And I hardly ever talk to my parents. I'm a terrible daughter.

Why. Why. *Why?*

I pace around the room. Unwanted thoughts keep rushing through my mind and my chest feels hollow and it hurts to breathe. I visualize putting my insecurities in a box, locking it up, and throwing it into the ocean, where it can't hurt me, but that doesn't help.

I should not be alone right now.

I pick up my phone to call Naomi. It might be a little late for her to come over, but she'll come if I need her. We can talk on the phone for a few minutes first, and maybe that will be enough to calm me down.

Or Julian! Nothing is better than feeling his arms around me. That will help me feel more like myself.

Okay. That's the plan. Call Julian and get him to come over. Simple plan. I can do it.

I pull up his contact information and dial. It rings…and rings…and rings…

Please, Julian, pick up. I need you.

…and then it goes to voicemail.

I end the call and send him a text rather than leave a voicemail.

It's fine. It really is. It's nine o'clock at night, so he shouldn't be at work, but maybe he's in the shower. He'll call me back soon.

I continue to pace, but my legs feel like lead. They're too heavy. This is too much work.

I collapse on the couch and call Julian again.

Still no answer.

Dammit.

It's okay. I can do this. I'll wait another ten minutes. Surely he'll call within ten minutes, and if not, I'll call Naomi. It's okay.

I manage another ten minutes, but when I call Julian again, I get voicemail.

Hmm. Maybe he had a work dinner, although wouldn't he have told me when I saw him at lunchtime?

But he didn't, and that's okay.

I don't deserve to have a boyfriend anyway.

I tremble and let it all wash over me, a wave slamming against the shore. Even if I do deserve to have a boyfriend, which is what Naomi would say, I *can't* have one. It's not safe for me.

Look at me. I'm a fucking wreck. I may have two degrees, but I'm an idiot who can't even read right now and can't stop all these awful thoughts from running through my mind. If something bad had happened, like a relative died or a parent was diagnosed with cancer, it would be reasonable for me to need his comfort.

Except I'm a fucking wreck over nothing. Planning a surprise lunchtime visit for Julian and having it not go as hoped—that was a little disappointing, but no big deal. Googling his ex and realizing she's successful and gorgeous was irritating, but they seem to be over each other, so no biggie, right?

Fuck, I'm so unstable.

It's not safe for me to have a boyfriend because no man is going to tolerate a woman like me. If I responded to medication and therapy, maybe it would be different, but my depression is so special that it resists treatment, so I'm stuck like this.

Who the fuck doesn't respond to therapy? What's wrong with me?

Inevitably, any boyfriend would break up with me, like Dane did. And that destroyed me. It tipped me over the edge.

I cannot survive that again.

I have to end this before it's too late.

At that thought, a sense of peace descends on me. I curl up on the couch, my mind blank. I still feel like crap, but at least my thoughts aren't coming rapid-fire anymore.

I have to break up with Julian. That's just the reality of the situation.

But I love him.

There's an unbearable hollowness in my chest, and my brain feels like it's stuffed with straw, but even through all that, I know I love him. It would be foolish to think this will be easy. However, it'll be easier to do it now than to deal with him leaving me in a couple months.

I snuggle up under the blanket and hug myself tight. The phone rings, and I jump in surprise, but I don't answer it. It's probably Julian, and I can't deal with that now. Tomorrow, I'll see him—we have plans to eat dinner together—and I'll end this.

When he asked me if we could be together, I never should have said yes, but what's done is done, and now I have to fix it.

There are quieter voices in my head, telling me that maybe it will all work out and we can be together and he won't leave me.

But I can't be seduced by that fantasy again.

It's a fantasy, nothing more.

[26]

JULIAN

I GET home at seven o'clock on Wednesday, which isn't bad. I was at the office for less than twelve hours, and I won't do any work tonight. I'll eat the meal Elena has prepared for me, text Courtney, watch some TV, and read a little before bed. I might even get to bed by ten, and that'll give me a solid seven hours of sleep.

How about that.

I eat dinner, and I'm just about to turn on the TV when there's a loud banging at the door.

I open it up. It's Vince. He staggers into my condo and sways as he walks to my couch.

"Too much tequila," he says. "Couldn't seem to stop. Was doing shots off a girl's stomach."

I don't know if that's true, but he's definitely drunk.

He tries to sit down on the couch but ends up falling to the floor. He makes it on his second attempt.

I go to the kitchen and pour him a glass of water, but he waves it away with a hiccup. "Can't keep anything down."

Dear God.

I grab a garbage can and put it next to him. "If you're going to puke, try to do it in there."

He nods, then rests his head on the armrest. "I hate my life," he says, in the most sorrowful voice. "I hate it. You were right. I'm not okay."

"Do you regret selling your company?"

"No." He hiccups or burps—I'm not sure which. "I didn't want it anymore. Wanted more time for hookers and blow."

"Vince, be serious." Yes, he's drunk, but perhaps this is my best chance of getting him to talk honestly.

"It's true. Sort of. Wanted to have a life. Less stress. More time for doing nothing and dicking around, more time for girls. Don't worry, I always use protection."

"Thank God," I mutter.

"Hey, the room is spinning. I didn't know your fancy condo *revolved.*"

"Nothing is spinning. You've just had too much to drink."

Vince throws an arm over his eyes. "I feel so unfulfilled." He laughs a truly miserable laugh. "Listen to the words I'm using. Such bullshit."

"What do you want to do with your life?"

"Don't know. Didn't want the company anymore, but didn't think I'd be so bored. I..." He looks like he's going to hurl. I thrust the garbage can in front of him just in time.

I do not have much experience with drunks—and that includes myself. It's been years since I had more than three drinks in a night. I don't like feeling out of control, and I definitely don't like feeling sick the next day.

He puts the garbage can down. "There. I think I'm done. I feel a little better now."

"You have vomit on your chin." I return to the kitchen to get some paper towels. I hand them to him so he can clean himself up, then sit down on the chair beside him. "Why did you come to my place?"

"Dunno. I like pissing you off."

"I'm aware of that."

"You're my best friend." He holds out his arms as though he wants a hug, but I don't go to him.

"That's sad," I say.

"I know. Pathetic. I'm pathetic."

"You just need to try a few things until you figure out what you like."

"Dunno why I'm asking you for help. You always knew what you wanted, and then you did it, and that's that."

This is true.

"Alone in a crowd," he says. "That's how I feel. I keep thinking if I surround myself with more people, I won't feel lonely. But it doesn't work. I'm lonely and bored and you're my best friend and now I want more tequila, though I'd settle for scotch."

"No. Drink the water instead."

He gives me the middle finger before drinking half the glass.

"Do you get drunk often?" I ask, rather afraid of the answer.

"Not this drunk."

Well, that's something.

"I'm jealous," he says. "You got a job. You got a girl."

"You have lots of girls, too, from the sounds of it."

He considers this for a moment. "Courtney is your *girlfriend*. It's different."

"Is that what you want? A girlfriend?"

"I don't know. No matter what I do, I'm bored."

"Much as I hate to say it, you're a very intelligent person who ran a successful tech company. It's hardly surprising you're bored now that you have nothing to challenge you. And it seems like you're also missing meaningful personal connections."

He looks at me as though I'm speaking Latin. "Too complicated for my simple brain."

I roll my eyes. "Okay. We'll talk when you're sober."

"Can I stay the night? I don't want to go home. We can paint our nails and listen to Katy Perry!"

I sigh. "You can stay the night, but this is not a sleepover party."

Settling back on the couch, he burps and closes his eyes.

Well, I'll leave him alone for a bit. I go to the kitchen and grab my phone off the table.

Three missed calls, all from Courtney. A text message that says, *Call me*, sent fifteen minutes ago. I know she wouldn't call me three times in twenty minutes unless it was urgent.

Shit.

I remember when she tripped on the stairs and lay in a heap on the floor. Her tears and blotchy face. Her flat voice.

I know exactly what happened to Courtney, and she needs me.

I call her, but there's no answer.

Shit. She shouldn't be alone. I need to go to her.

I hurry to the living room and glance at Vince. He's snoring like a freight train. I don't want him to wake up alone, since he's not doing well, so I call Cedric and ask him to check on Vince. Then I hurry to Courtney's.

When Courtney opens the door to her apartment, she's wrapped in a fuzzy blanket—even though it's summer—and her face is shuttered.

"Hey," she says quietly, her voice dull.

I step inside and wrap her in my arms. It hurts so much to see her like this, without her usual spark and joy.

"I had a meltdown," she explains. "That's why I tried to call you. I thought you could hold me."

"I'm here now." I lead her to the couch. "I'm so sorry. I didn't hear the phone. Vince came over, and he's drunk and not in a good place. My phone was in the other room and... I'm sorry. About lunch, too. I wish I could have eaten with you."

"It's okay. I understand. I would have done the same for Naomi. Not to worry."

But her next words, spoken after we cuddle for a few minutes, make my heart drop.

"I think we should break up," she says, pulling away from me.

"What?" I couldn't have heard that correctly.

"I think we should break up. We *have* to break up."

I'm shaking my head before she can finish speaking. Apparently I did hear her properly the first time. "You're just saying that because you had a bad evening. You don't really mean it."

"Oh, so now you think I'm crazy and you won't listen to me?"

What?

"I never said you were crazy, but you're not yourself now. You shouldn't make rash decisions." She won't seriously think this is a good idea tomorrow, will she?

"I have news for you, Julian. This *is* me. This is who I am."

"No, it's just your depression talking."

Her eyes flash.

I've read a lot about depression in the past week. I know it can twist your thinking, and I know some people find it helpful to think of their depression as a separate entity from them.

But it appears I've said the wrong thing.

"How dare you," she says, jumping up. "When you're depressed, that's all anyone says to you. 'It's just your depression talking.' Nobody believes anything you say. They just assume you're always full of shit."

I hold up my hands and get to my feet. "I'm not saying that, but right now—"

"Tomorrow, I'll still think the same thing. We shouldn't be together. When you asked to keep seeing me after our two weeks were up, I knew it was a bad idea. I just couldn't stop myself from saying yes because I like you a lot. But it was foolish of me. You think you can handle me now, but you're going to break up with me like Dane did because you won't be able to handle it when I'm sick for months at a time."

"No." I shake my head vehemently. "I won't break up with you. I love you."

I didn't want the first time I said those words to be in anger, but there it is.

Now she's the one shaking her head. "You don't truly love me."

Her words pierce my heart. She doesn't understand how wrong she is.

I know who I am. A man who loves her more than anything.

Goddammit. "You're mad at me for not believing what you say, but you won't believe what I say, either. Courtney, I mean it. I do love you."

"You love the woman who enjoys gingerbread lattes and wandering around the city."

"Yes. That's you."

"Sometimes it's me."

"Your depression is not *you*."

"I can't separate myself from my mental illness. It's a part of me."

"We'll fix it," I say. "We'll get you healthy again. I have resources that you don't. We can figure it out. Depression is a treatable illness."

"You don't understand. You think you can throw money at any problem and fix it, but it's not like that. I told you, I tried. I tried so goddamn hard, believe me. I tried every drug they suggested, even though none of them worked and some of them had awful side effects." There are tears in her lashes. "You know how exhausting it is to keep trying new treatments and having them fail? To have your hopes crushed over and over? I refuse to try any more drugs."

"Therapy. It's not generally covered under provincial health-care and it can get expensive, but—"

"I've tried. I saw literally every counselor at the universities I attended."

"*Counselor*. They probably weren't psychologists with PhDs."

"A couple of them were. And you know what? Talking about my problems isn't helpful for me—it just makes me more depressed. Therapy was essentially a regularly-scheduled ugly cry session. I'm not kidding. It's awful. I've even been told I'm too sick for therapy at times."

"You just haven't found the right therapist, and I—"

"You don't get it." She's shaking. Her voice is shaking, too, but it's still clear. "You really don't get it. I'm the one who's had to live through endless treatments that always fail. Not you."

She's right, of course. This is her life, her experience, but I refuse to accept that her problem cannot be fixed. It's too painful for me to contemplate. She has to keep trying.

I take her hands in mine. She jerks away.

"You know when I finally got better the last two times?" she asks. "When I gave up on treatment. I told you that, didn't I? When I gave up, it felt like a weight had been lifted off my shoulders—one less thing to worry about. Trying to get better was just too stressful." She exhales unsteadily. "This time, I'm not going to try. I don't need you to throw money at me and pay for more therapy. What I need is support. Compassion. But I know it's ridiculous to expect any man to put up with my untreatable mental illness. It's a one-sided relationship."

"Once every five years."

"Maybe this time it won't go away."

"Don't say that. We'll get through it together. I will be there for you. You don't have to try any more anti-depressants, but there are other things—"

"I won't let anyone give me an electric shock twice a week or drill a hole in my head to implant a pacemaker. There are limits to what I will try, and I've reached them."

"You can't give up on everything." I want to shake her and

scream that it's just her depression talking, but I don't. "You can't give up on *us*."

"It's self-preservation."

"No!"

"I think you should leave, Julian."

"I guess I should. I should listen to you even though you're talking nonsense right now."

"That's right. Brush off everything I say as nonsense because I'm mentally ill."

I'm so angry. At Courtney, at all the people who couldn't help her, at the ex who made her believe she couldn't have a relationship. But I see no way out of this.

So I leave.

[27]

COURTNEY

WHEN JULIAN WALKS OUT, I slide to the floor, my back against the door. I press my hands to my eyes, but I don't cry.

I just sit there.

On one hand, I'm relieved. It's finally over, like I wanted.

On the other hand…

Well, this isn't actually what I wanted, because I love Julian and he loves me, but it's what had to happen, and now I can move on with my life. That's good, right?

He doesn't get it, and that's okay. He can't get it because he hasn't lived with mental illness for decades, unlike me. He thinks depression is something that's treatable for everyone, but it's not like that for all of us. It's just a part of our lives, as much as we hate it.

I feel calmer now. I did what I had to do.

～

The next day, I have a gingerbread latte at lunch. I deserve a reward.

I get only the slightest pleasure out of the latte, but it's still there, that sliver of pleasure, and it's better than nothing.

This is my life. It's mine to figure out, and I can do it, but having Julian around would just confuse matters and blow up in my face at the most inconvenient time.

Then I remember the day he came up to me at Chris's Coffee Shop. Our banter, the way he told me I was perfect. There's a lump in my throat, and I grab my latte and run out of the coffee shop. It's near City Hall, and I see the plaques that commemorate Toronto's first Chinatown, but that reminds me of Julian, too.

He's ruined Toronto for me.

We had so many good times together, both here and in Montreal. Eating pineapple buns and gelato. Kissing in the rain. Going to nice restaurants. Trying not to jump each other in public. I remember entering his bedroom, wearing only his blue dress shirt... He said he would take care of me.

And he did. He took care of me then and when I had a meltdown during his fancy home-cooked meal. It was so nice to have someone there for me, someone to hold me. It was nice not to be completely reliant upon my sister for help.

If he could always give that to me when I was down, if I knew I could always count on him, it probably would make my depressive episodes a little less severe and easier to handle.

However, Julian would not be able to stay. He doesn't really get what it's like. He can't accept that my depression is untreatable; he believes he can fix me.

But he can't.

God, I do love him, even if he doesn't fully understand me.

I walk back to the lab with my lukewarm latte. I feel a little shaky, off-balance, and I hate that, but I try to be nice to myself. I just had a breakup, and even though Julian and I were only together for a short period of time, he still means so much to me. That won't go away overnight.

What will improve my mood?

I text Lydia to see if today would be a good day to visit Heather.

~

My niece is in a great mood when I arrive after work. She's just been fed, and she gurgles happily. She's more responsive now. When I shake a toy on one side of her head, she actually looks in that direction. All these tiny milestones that I never would have thought of, but she's a little different every time I see her.

"Why don't I take her for a walk?" I suggest.

Lydia tells me to use the baby carrier instead of the stroller because Heather has been fussy in the stroller lately. I get set up with the baby carrier with Heather facing toward me, and we set out on our walk around the neighborhood. I figure twenty minutes, maybe half an hour. Perhaps Heather will fall asleep.

"Let's go," I say as we head down the front steps. "Baby Heather and Aunt Courtney on a great big adventure!"

She makes some noises and moves her hands around in response.

Okay, this is good. Me and a happy baby.

But as I walk down the street, I'm overcome with a wave of sadness. I love my niece, but I can't have a baby of my own because I can't have a relationship.

Sure, technically, I could have a baby without a relationship, but I think I would really struggle as a single mother, given my mental health problems, which probably also put me at a higher risk of postpartum depression. I doubt it would be a good idea for me to set out on that path. If I were to have a baby, I'd want to at least try to have a serious relationship.

Unfortunately, that's out of the question.

There might be a miniscule chance that I could make a relationship work, but it's not worth the risk, not when it could kill me.

God, I wish I could have a baby. Just one, maybe two. Not a huge family, but a family nonetheless.

"It's okay," I say to Heather, trying to sound upbeat. "I have you! I'm your *fun* aunt."

Will and Naomi will probably have kids, too. I'll have a few nieces and nephews. It'll be good enough.

Dammit, I miss Julian. He was adorable with Heather.

Deep breaths. It's okay. I can do this.

I turn a corner and head toward the park. Heather makes some more noises, and then her face scrunches up and she begins to wail at the top of her lungs.

"Shh." I walk with more of a bounce in my step. "It's okay! Mama's not here, but you'll see her soon."

Heather is quiet for a moment, looking at me skeptically, then begins to wail again.

"We're at the park! So many children on the playground. Soon you'll be able to run around with them. Won't that be fun?"

Heather apparently doesn't think so. She keeps crying.

She was happy just a few minutes ago. What did I do wrong? Or maybe she needs to be changed? I don't know.

A few tears slide down my cheeks. Her tears are contagious.

"It's okay." I say that for my benefit as well as Heather's.

It's okay.

It's just a crying baby; it's not like she cries only for me.

I bounce her up and down as we walk around the park. She still hasn't stopped crying by the time we're finished, so I head back to the house rather than taking her on a longer walk.

Heather seems happier once she's out of the carrier, so perhaps that was the problem. Perhaps she's changed her mind about the stroller versus carrier issue, just like Naomi changed her mind about eggs multiple times a week when she was little.

The shower is running upstairs. A few minutes later, Lydia comes down with a towel wrapped around her head.

"Will you be okay with Heather while I cook dinner?" she asks.

"Sure. We're good."

I find a board book on the coffee table and start reading it to my niece. She doesn't start crying again—and neither do I—and for now, that's all I can ask.

For the next few days, Julian is never far from my mind, despite my efforts to distract myself. I miss him so much.

If only I were someone other than who I am.

WHEN I GET home from work at three o'clock on Saturday, I go up to my rooftop patio with a beer, as well as my laptop and the flash drive Courtney gave me on Wednesday. I'm finally going to look at whatever is on it.

The last few days have seemed interminable. Twelve-hour days at work feel like twenty-four-hour days. I haven't been sleeping much, either, maybe three or four hours a night.

Life was better with Courtney.

I turn on the laptop. It takes me several tries to get the fucking flash drive into the USB port because I am a fucking sleep-deprived wreck. There's a single folder on the flash drive, labeled "photos," and I open it.

It's all the pictures from my two-week holiday. Some were taken on my phone, some on hers. The first one is of me lying on my back in Riverdale Park, staring up at the sky and cursing, from the looks of it.

I manage a chuckle.

There are pictures of gelato and tapas…and the phallic cactus, of course. There are a few pictures of the two of us, which

Courtney took using her selfie stick. I told her selfie sticks were an abomination, but I let her do it anyway. Just a few times. In one of these pictures, we're sitting on the rooftop patio, like I am now, with drinks in our hands.

We had so many good times together.

And now it's over.

I chug half my beer, then close my eyes and tip my head toward the sun.

"He's sleeping on the patio, and he's not wearing a shirt. Has this become a regular occurrence?"

"Another bottle of Labatt 50. My God, he has bad taste."

"Well, he's getting old."

"True, true."

Not this again.

I open my eyes. My brothers are standing before me. I left a key for Cedric when I asked him to check on Vince the other day —I guess they let themselves in.

"I'm not that old," I mutter. "Now leave me in peace."

"Ooh, he's grumpy," Vince says. "Understandable, since his girlfriend dumped him."

"Where the hell did you hear that?" I ask.

"I texted Courtney to invite her to your birthday party, and she informed me of the breakup."

I never should have let them become friends. "My birthday isn't for another month."

"I know, but I have nothing to do with my life, so I'm planning you a big party. How do you feel about clowns?"

Dear God.

I pinch the bridge of my nose. "You're the one who was drunk off his ass on Wednesday. I think we should be talking about your problems rather than my breakup."

"You'll be happy to know that I made an appointment with a therapist, so you and I don't need to have any more heart-to-heart talks. Now, back to clowns. Is that a no? How would you feel about a petting zoo?"

"I thought you said I was getting old. Instead, you're treating me like a toddler."

"He really is grumpy," Cedric says.

"Can you please stop talking about me like I'm not here?"

Vince picks up my laptop, which is sitting on the table next to me. "Look at all these happy pictures. Joey sure looks dapper in this one. Were you mooning and crying over them before you fell asleep?"

"Courtney gave me the flash drive on Wednesday. I just wanted to see what was on it."

Vince and Cedric exchange a look.

"I thought you two broke up on Wednesday?" Vince says.

"We did. This was earlier. She came to my office with lunch, pineapple buns, and the flash drive, but unfortunately, I had to rush off to a meeting three minutes later. Then when your sorry ass was drunk on my couch, she called me three times in twenty minutes, and I missed the calls. That's why I went over while you were asleep."

Vince frowns. "She broke up with you because you were too busy comforting your drunk brother to answer her calls?"

I run a hand through my hair. "She claimed she understood, but then she said we couldn't be together anymore, and we had a fight..."

"About what? Not about me, I hope."

"No." I want to talk to someone about Courtney's depression, but it's her story to tell, and she hasn't given me permission to talk to other people about it. I settle on being vague. "She has some...issues. I'm not comfortable sharing the details. There are treatments available, but she's tried many of them, and they haven't worked. So she believes she's stuck with this problem. I said I couldn't bear to see her suffer, and surely we would be able to find something, since money isn't a barrier for me…"

Cedric snorts. "Yeah. We know."

"…and she said I didn't understand how exhausting it was to keep trying things and having them fail." I scrub my hands over my face.

"Not everyone wants you to fix their problems."

"I really want to fix her problem. It hurts her so much."

"What does *she* want from you?" Vince asks.

"Support and compassion."

"Surely you can give her those, no? You don't need to go into every situation with a hammer and a drill. Although drilling is—"

"Shut up," I say, a little too forcefully, but Vince just shrugs. "Her ex dumped her when she was at her worst, and so she thinks it's too much to expect someone to put up with her when she's unwell. She doesn't believe she can have a relationship."

"Tell her you love her," Cedric say. "I hear that's the solution to a lot of problems with women. Not that I know from personal experience, but I read it in a book once."

"I already did that. Though I may have been angry at the time."

It suddenly strikes me as comical that my brothers are trying to help me with this. Neither of them knows anything about relationships, despite being in their thirties. I doubt we'll make any progress here. I'd rather go back to drinking my old man beer in peace, then perhaps have another nap.

"So you do love her," Vince says. "I suspected as much. You made a point of introducing her to Cedric, after all."

"And she knows *you* because I didn't have a choice in the matter," I grumble. "You barged in at eight o'clock in the morning after your orgy."

"She kept you away from the office for two weeks. I didn't think it was possible, but she did it. You even had fun. She's a miracle worker."

"Yes, she is."

"And you want to be there for her in sickness and in health."

"Yes."

"So you want to get married."

Do I?

I don't have to think too hard. I know the answer.

"Eventually," I say, "but that seems unlikely, considering she dumped me."

"If she's the woman you want to marry," Vince says, "you shouldn't give up because you had one argument."

"She was very clear on the matter."

"Because she doesn't believe you can give her this support and compassion stuff, since her ex fucked with her head. So all you have to do is show her that you're good for it."

"Thanks, genius."

"You're not taking me seriously. I mean it. You show her that you're a compassionate, supportive guy who won't bail when times get tough. Which is the truth."

I raise my eyebrows. "Do you actually believe that?"

He shrugs. "Why do you think I come here to bug you all the time? You're nice guy under all that no-nonsense workaholic veneer."

"You called me your best friend on Wednesday."

Cedric puts a hand to his chest. "What about me?"

Vince ignores him. "All is not lost. You just need a really great plan. Like a petting zoo *and* a clown."

"Jesus Christ," I mutter.

"You know I'm a genius. You called me that a minute ago."

Irritating little brothers.

"Your ideas suck." I turn to Cedric. "You're the writer. You're supposed to be creative."

"Sorry, I got nothing."

Vince slaps me on the back. "You need to figure it out yourself." He jerks Cedric's arm forward. "I think we've outstayed our usefulness. Birthday boy here needs to drink his old man beer and do some thinking."

"My birthday isn't for another month!"

"Details, details. By the way, Po Po is coming by tonight. She was very concerned when she heard about your breakup."

"Did you really need to broadcast it to the whole world?" I ask.

"Yes, yes, I did," Vince says cheerfully as he and Cedric head down the stairs.

I have another sip of my beer and close my eyes, grateful to have some peace and quiet at last. But I can't go back to sleep. My busy mind won't allow it.

I'm not angry at Courtney. I know she was just doing what she felt she needed to do. I know she was trying to save herself.

I need to show her that she doesn't have to do it all alone.

"I don't need *jook*," I say, "and I certainly don't need to learn how to make it."

"You're sick," Po Po says. "You need *jook*."

"I'm not sick, and I'm not in the mood for it." Right now, I'd much prefer a greasy burger and fries over rice porridge.

"Heartbroken, sick." She waves her bony hand in the air as she putters around my kitchen. "Same thing. But you will make *jook* and get healthy, and then you will win her back!" She beams at me.

"Don't get your hopes up."

"Vince said you would do it."

"Why do you listen to anything Vince says?"

Po Po pulls out a large pot. "I'm eighty-nine. Want great-grandchildren, and Courtney is a nice Chinese girl who helps you have fun. You must make this work. Then you can cook her *jook* when she's pregnant. When I was pregnant, I could not keep much down. Just *jook*."

I stare at her. This is all a bit much. "You're getting ahead of yourself."

"I know. First I must plan the wedding."

"No. You'll make the entire playlist Chinese opera."

She chuckles. Then she raises a finger in the air, as if to make an important declaration. "You must make Courtney happy. If I do not hear this by next Saturday, I will come to your office every day. Play Chinese opera, bring new girl. Until you're so annoyed, you'll do anything to get Courtney back."

I've blocked off Sunday morning in my calendar for "brainstorming."

As in, brainstorming ways to get Courtney Kwan back.

I don't know if this will work. Maybe I'll end up being subjected to endless opera music and a parade of eligible Chinese women.

It better work.

Because I really love Courtney.

And I really hate Chinese opera.

I stare at the blank sheet of paper, then finally write down one thing: Call Naomi. Courtney's close with her sister. Maybe she can help me.

But I think I should have some kind of plan in place before I get to that step.

I tell myself not to get distracted, but soon I'm turning on my laptop and looking through all the pictures again. I particularly like the one I took of her laughing when we were at Mosaic. She's so luminous.

The photos give me one idea, and I write it down on the sheet of paper. Just looking at the word makes me groan, but it *is* a pretty good idea that requires only a little damage to my dignity and involves neither clowns nor a petting zoo.

However, I'm not a workaholic for nothing, and I write down forty-seven other ideas in the next hour. My brothers are right. I need to try.

I like a few of the ideas, but I think the key is to ask Courtney what she needs and listen to her. Develop a plan together to deal with her depression so I know exactly how to support her. Naomi might be able to give me some input, but I need to have a proper discussion with Courtney when neither of us is angry, when I really listen to everything she says. She's the one who's lived with this for years, which is such a painful thought, but it's the unfortunate truth. She's the one who's developed strategies to deal with it. Not me.

I'm going to do everything I can for her, if only she'll let me.

I realize now that, although I thought I was a hundred percent committed to this relationship before, it wasn't quite true. I think part of the reason I struggled with my previous relationships is that I was subconsciously afraid to get too invested in someone, fearing it would take away from my work and my ability to be the responsible son. Even once I decided to give it a go with Courtney, some of that feeling remained.

But no longer.

I am completely committed to her. She is my priority, and that doesn't scare me at all.

She also makes me feel like anything is possible. I know I can still do a good job of running the company; however, I won't allow it to take over my life.

I'm going to need a little help, though. I have to stop trying to do everything on my own. It's not possible. And besides, life is meaningless if I have no time for anything but work, and if I keep it up, I could easily burn out before I'm forty.

There's something I'd like to talk to my dad about, and as luck would have it, my parents arrive at my door only five minutes later.

I want to have a chat with my father, but not like this. Not when my parents are loaded down with food and looking at me like I'm an injured wild animal.

"Vince said Courtney broke up with you," Mom says.

"You don't need to bring me a truck full of food. I can take care of myself, plus I already have a pot of *jook,* thanks to Po Po."

"The only girlfriend you've had in ages, and it doesn't even last a month!" Mom clucks her tongue, then starts putting the food on the kitchen island. "But Vince says you'll fix it. Please do. We like Courtney."

"I'll try." I pause. "Dad, I have to ask you something. I'd like if you could come back to work—"

"Yes," he says, before I finish.

"Thank heavens!" Mom says, looking up at the ceiling with her hands clasped.

"Just a couple days a week," I say, "in an advisory position. Not full-time of course, and *I* will still be in charge, but I could use some help. I don't want to work eighty-hour weeks on a regular basis."

I have a lot of responsibilities, and I'll never work only forty hours a week, but I can do better. Perhaps it's also time to consider re-organizing senior management. I'll still be CEO, but I don't need to be CEO *and* president. Someone else can focus on overseeing the day-to-day operations.

Dad nods. "I was bored at home. I have my work at the Toronto Chinese-Canadian Center, of course, but I still had too much free time. It was nice being back at the office. I don't need to play golf five times a week."

"He's been driving me up the wall," Mom says.

He turns to her. "It hasn't been that bad. I thought you liked having me around."

"Not *that* much."

A thought occurs to me. "Mom, was the whole forcing-me-to-take-a-vacation thing because you wanted Dad to go into the office so he wouldn't be around as much?"

"Of course not! It was because I was worried about you working such long hours." She pauses and takes my hands. "You were always serious and a hard worker, even as a child. You seemed older than your years. I think we depended on you too much at times, and after your father's heart attack…"

Yes, my workaholic tendencies got even worse after I became CEO. I was suddenly thrust into a position I wasn't quite prepared for. I had a lot to learn, and I was determined to make my family proud. Perhaps I was also trying to distract myself from thinking about my father's health.

But it's been three years now, and things are running pretty smoothly.

"Maybe we expected too much of you when you were younger," Dad said. "You took those expectations so seriously, but we don't want success to come at the expense of everything else."

I nod. "I understand that now."

"I worked too hard at times, too. Didn't have enough time for my family. After my heart attack, I came to see things a little differently. We're proud of what you've accomplished, Julian. Don't ever doubt that."

"Yes," Mom says. "We're very proud."

I'm glad to hear that, but more importantly, I'm glad I've figured out exactly what I want.

I squeeze my mother's hands. "I'll do better at having a balanced life now, I promise."

She smiles at me before stepping back and continuing to unload the food. "Your dad's taken up carpentry, did you know? He's terrible at it."

"Am not," Dad says.

"You are. That chair broke the first time I sat on it!"

As my parents bicker, my thoughts wander back to Courtney.

I'll cut down on my hours even further, at least for the next few months, so I can help her in any way she needs.

I WAS GOING TO BAKE, but that reminded me of Julian.

I was going to go for a walk and lie on the grass in Riverdale Park, but that also reminded me of Julian.

So, instead, I'm sitting on my couch alone, eating ice cream from the tub.

Ha. No. I'm not that much of a stereotype.

I'm actually looking at pictures of terrariums online to give myself ideas. I figure making a terrarium will be a nice little project to distract me. But then a particularly phallic cactus reminds me of Joey, which in turn makes me think of Julian. I can't help thinking of him, even when I try not to.

Damn.

My phone rings.

"It's me," Dad says. "I'm downstairs. Can you buzz me up?"

I do as he asks, and then I start freaking out.

Dad would never visit me without warning on a Sunday morning. What's going on? Is Mom with him...or did something happen to her? I pace my living room until he knocks on the door, and I immediately pull it open.

"What's wrong?" I ask.

He frowns. "Nothing's wrong."

"Then why are you here? It's Sunday morning."

"I'm aware of what time it is."

He sits down heavily on my couch, his face a mask of concentration, his gaze on his hands. My father is nearly seventy, and his hair has been gray for a while. He's also thinner than he used to be, I notice now. I take a seat on the chair across from him.

"I'm sorry," he says at last.

"For what?" I have no idea what we're talking about.

"For refusing to accept that you were sick."

Oh.

"Jeremy came to talk to me." Dad's not looking at me—I think that's too difficult for him. "He said we screwed up. Me, him, and your mother. Though I think it started with me. I guess I thought...maybe if I denied it, it wouldn't be true. You'd snap out of it. Be yourself again."

"Don't you hear how ridiculous that sounds?"

"I know." He nods. "I know." He looks down at the floor. "My father...you never knew him because he died when he was forty-eight. He threw himself in front of a train. Before that, he wasn't well. Depressed, maybe, but we didn't call it that."

"Aunt Darlene told me."

"Oh." He pauses. "I don't let myself think about it, but when you were..." He makes a vague gesture with his hands. "I had to think about it again, and I couldn't deal with it."

"Maybe if I'd gotten proper help earlier, it would have been easier. But the first time, I was only sixteen. I needed my parents to help me get treatment, and you dismissed it. Honestly, I wasn't surprised. I hadn't wanted to tell you in the first place because I knew how you'd react. And when I was in university..." I shake my head. I don't want to talk about that.

He didn't even visit me in the hospital. Naomi came every day, and Mom and Jeremy came once, but Dad never did.

I swallow. "Thank you for the apology. It doesn't make everything okay, though."

"I know. I will do better in the future if it happens again."

"It's starting. I can feel it. Every five years…"

"Come here."

I sit beside him on the couch. He places his hand on my shoulder, which is the most affection he's shown me since I was sixteen. When I shed a few tears, I can tell he's uncomfortable, but he stays, sitting beside me.

It will never be perfect between us, and it's sad that he wouldn't change until he heard it from Jeremy.

Still, it's something.

~

"Are you okay?" Bethany asks as we head to the banh mi restaurant together.

Usually we have lunch on Friday, but she had to cancel because her son needed to go to the doctor, so we're doing Monday instead.

"Julian and I broke up," I say.

"Oh no! I'm so sorry."

I don't tell her that it was my doing, that I feel like I can't be in any relationship at all. But do I say, "I have some problems with clinical depression."

I tell her a bit about my history with mental illness. I haven't told anyone—other than Julian—in a long time. I don't want everyone in my life to know about it, but I want Bethany, my closest friend at work, to know.

I'm not going to lean on her much, and I'm not going to talk to her about my problems on a regular basis—those conversations usually just makes me feel like shit anyway. But it's easier now that she knows the truth and is still standing here next to me.

She gives me a quick hug when we're in line at the banh mi restaurant.

"What are you getting today?" she asks.

It's a joke we have, since I always get the same thing.

"Hmm." I pretend to think real hard. "Maybe the chicken. Or the beef. But I hear the grilled pork is really good. Or maybe I'll do something completely different and order the pork belly..."

I don't need much from most people, and I'm aware of how difficult it is to be around me when I'm unwell. I just need Bethany to still be my once-a-week lunch friend. I need to know my father isn't going to deny that I'm sick.

The little things add up.

Wednesday evening, I'm at Naomi's apartment, and we're sharing a bottle of wine as we plan our trip to New York. I'm excited for our trip, but it's tinged with sadness because I can't stop thinking of Julian. He's the reason we're able to go.

When I saw Naomi last Thursday, I told her what happened, but she didn't make me talk about it much. Today, however, is a different story.

She puts aside her laptop and fiddles with her wine glass. "I think you're wrong when you say you can't have a relationship."

I stiffen. "It's not safe for me."

"You can't only do things that are safe."

"Obviously I have to take some risks in life, but this one isn't worth it. I'll *die* if we get too close and then he breaks up with me."

"You will not die," she says, taking my hand. "I will look after you, I promise."

"But there's no treatment for my depression. It doesn't respond to anything."

"You can be kept safe in a crisis situation." She pauses. "It wouldn't have been a good idea to start dating soon after Dane, I agree, but it's been ten years since you had a relationship, not counting the past few weeks. I think you're punishing yourself. This isn't only about your fear that it won't work out and will turn out like last time. I believe you're also letting your depression tell you that you don't deserve a relationship."

I shake my head. "No. It's not like that."

"I hate to say this, because I know you don't like the phrase, but when you tell me you can't be in a relationship, I think, 'It's just your depression talking.' You're letting your negative self-talk get the better of you. You deserve to have someone who cares for you like that. You *can* have a relationship, and maybe you'll never break up."

"But—"

"You think he can't handle your problems? He cares for you very much, and we all have problems."

"Mine aren't the normal kind of problems."

"They're far from *un*common. It's not a hardship to be with you, Courtney. You have to stop thinking like that. There will be hard times, yes, but you'll get through them. Plus, the man is a CEO. I'm sure he's used to handling problems."

I sigh and put my face in my hands.

I don't know, I don't know.

If this were coming from anyone but Naomi, I wouldn't even consider it. But my sister is the one person who's always been there for me, always been supportive. If she thinks I'm punishing myself, maybe she's right. If she thinks it's not too much to expect a man to handle me when I'm depressed, maybe it's true. It's hard to wrap my mind around that possibility, but for the first time in a long time, it's a possibility.

"You focus on what you consider the difficult parts of being with you," Naomi says, "but those aren't what come to mind when I think of my sister. I don't consider you a difficult person. You're unlucky to have the problems you have, but a man who truly loves you isn't going to desert you because of something beyond your control. It's not like you've refused to get help. You've tried lots of treatments, and you put a lot of effort into keeping yourself mentally healthy, always considering whether everything you do is good for you. It's painful to see you throw something like this away when it's clear you love Julian and he loves you."

"Has he talked to you since last Wednesday?"

She shrugs. "He might have."

"What did he say?"

Naomi pours herself some more wine. "I'm not telling."

I pull the wine glass out of her hand. "I'm not giving this back until you do."

"Fine. Be that way." She grabs my mostly-full wine glass from the table and takes a gulp.

I laugh and have a sip of her wine.

"Just think about it," she says. "Please."

"I will," I say, and I do mean it.

I SIT DOWN on my recliner with a cup of tea, two gingersnap cookies, and a chick lit novel. I dip the edge of a cookie in the tea and take a bite, and I can't help but smile. It's delicious. A few years ago, I tried several brands of gingersnaps and figured out which one was best, and that's all I've bought ever since.

Tea, cookies, and a book, plus a long week of work behind me. I've already finished my laundry and tidied up my apartment.

Life is good.

But there's an ache in my heart. Part of me feels dull and dead inside. I might be able to enjoy myself, but I'm not fully present.

I keep wondering if Naomi is right.

I'm prone to negative self-talk, and sometimes my behavior is self-defeating. Yet that was never how I saw my refusal to consider another relationship. I told myself I was being smart and sensible, but maybe my mind was twisting everything around. After all, my mind does malfunction at times.

And that's okay. I do not need to be perfect.

My phone rings. I grab it off the table beside me, expecting it to be Naomi, but it's not.

"It's Julian. Could you buzz me up?"

My heart nearly stops when I hear his voice.

"Yes," I whisper, and then I let him in downstairs.

I spend the next two minutes pacing my living room, freaking out in a different way than when my father came to visit me.

Julian is here.

My mind immediately jumps to unimportant reasons for his visit. Maybe I left a T-shirt or hairbrush behind.

But I know that's not the reason, even before I open the door and see him standing there with a terrarium, a large book, and a takeout cup that I know contains a gingerbread latte. He's wearing a suit, and his serious gaze is fixed on me.

"May I come in?" he asks.

I gesture him inside, and he puts everything on the coffee table before sitting down. If it were me, I probably would have dropped the latte and spilled it all over the floor, but Julian does so many things with ease. I take a seat beside him, my heart thumping from being so close to him after so long.

Well, it was only a little over a week, but it feels like longer.

He hands me the book. "This is for you."

The cover of the book is blue, with purple flowers and green vines and a few butterflies. There are no words on it.

I laugh as I realize what it is.

It's a scrapbook.

I open it up. There are two photos on the first page: one of Riverdale Park with downtown Toronto in the distance, and the other of Julian lying on the grass. There are paper frames around the photos, cut-out daisies along the bottom of the page, and the words "Riverdale Park" in purple letters. The next page says "Chinatown East" and includes a picture of Julian shoving a pineapple bun into his mouth.

"I wish I'd taken more photos of you," he says.

There are pictures of us eating gelato, drinking cocktails, and standing at the top of Mont Royal. He's printed out the pictures I gave him and turned them into a scrapbook, and I swear, every single page looks like it could be in a "How to Scrapbook" article.

"Did you take a class?" I ask, struggling to form words. "Private lessons?"

"No, I just poked around on the internet and went to a store to get some supplies. Paper and decorative punches and various other things."

I chuckle. "How long did this take? It looks like more than an afternoon's work."

"It doesn't matter," he says quietly. "It was worth it. I loved my two weeks off with you, and I want us to always remember them." He takes my hand and squeezes it, then gives me the gingerbread latte. I was just drinking tea a minute ago, but I'll never turn down a gingerbread latte.

He points to the terrarium. "I didn't make this myself, but I thought you'd like it. You can name the plants. I figured I'd leave that task to you." He runs a hand through his hair. "I made a list of forty-eight things I could do for you, and I probably could have stuck with one, but I didn't."

"Forty-eight," I repeat.

"Forty-eight. It's easy to think of gifts for you, but..." He pulls a pen out of his pocket, as well as a small spiral notebook with flowers on the cover. "Maybe this is the most important. You're going to tell me what I should do when you need support, which things will help in different situations. I promise, I'll do whatever you need, and I promise, it's not a hardship for me to do so. We just need a strategy, and you're in control of that, not me. I'm not going to tell you that you have to try every new drug that's been developed in the past five years, or that you should subject yourself to electroshock treatments. You're the expert on your health, not me. I do think maybe we could investigate psychotherapy options that might not have been available to you before, but you can say no. It's fine. You..." He cups my cheek. "You've lived with this for a long time, and I think it's amazing how you've managed to make the best of it and enjoy your life. But it doesn't mean you can't have a relationship. You can have me, and I promise to always be there for you. I'm sorry I got angry at you the other night, but I will do better and I think—I *know*—we can make it work." He manages a small smile. "I do not fail."

I feel vulnerable and raw and... I can't explain everything I feel, but I want to burst into tears and grin at the same time.

"You don't have to worry about me working all the time," he continues. "I've been a bit better since my forced vacation, and my dad is going to come back to work two days a week to help me."

I shake my head. "He doesn't have to do that."

"He wants to. My mom wants him to. I don't think men like my father enjoy total retirement. He couldn't work right after his heart attack, but he's healthy now, and he's driving my mom nuts at home. It's not like he'll be working full-time." Julian slips his hands through my hair. "Tell me we can try again, Courtney. I think you're wonderful. You did what everyone in my family thought was impossible: you kept me away from the office for more than two weeks and taught me how to have fun."

"That's hardly a miracle."

"I disagree. I was missing so much...until I met you. I love you." He fumbles with something in his pocket and then holds up a promise ring. It's white gold with a star made of small diamonds. "I promise I will not leave you. I will always be there for you, and I will always listen to you. You don't have to worry about this ending." He holds the ring to the tip of my ring finger. "May I?"

I nod, and he slides it on.

"It's okay," I whisper to myself. "I can do this." I look up at him. "That's how I talk to myself when I'm overwhelmed."

"And you're overwhelmed now—"

"In a good way. Don't worry." I wrap my arms around him. "I love you, too, and I deserve to love and be loved in return."

It's a big step for me to say those words.

We hold each other for a minute, and then he dips his head at the same time as I tilt my head up. We kiss slowly, savoring each other.

Even though Naomi put the idea in my head a few days ago, it's still hard to wrap my mind around it all. I can have this, even though I told myself for a decade that I couldn't. My depression hasn't been solved, but with Julian, I'm less scared of the next few months. I have him as well as my sister, and I have other people who will be there, too.

I am so lucky.

And I will be okay.

We'll have many more gingerbread lattes and pineapple buns. We'll bake chocolate chip cookies and eat the dough. We'll go on vacations—probably fancy ones, since Julian can afford it, not that I care, as long as I get to travel. Late-night conversations. Middle-of-the-night sex.

I'm still overwhelmed at the thought of all the things we'll do together, all the great moments we'll share.

And even when things aren't great, we'll have each other.

I pick up the notebook and pen, which Julian has placed on the coffee table, and stare at the blank paper, tears blurring my vision.

He thinks I'm the one who performed a miracle, but he did, too. He made me believe in myself in a way I never could before. He showed me that I'm a pretty damn amazing and desirable woman.

I have a CEO boyfriend now, and that might seem like the stuff of fairy tales, but I don't doubt we are right for each other.

"Could we do this later?" I ask, flipping through the blank pages of the notebook.

"Of course."

I climb onto his lap and bury my head against his shoulder.

It's such a pleasure to be held like this, but there's something that would make it even better.

I grab the package of gingersnaps from the table. I take one out, break off a piece, and feed it to him, and then he feeds the rest of it to me.

"Everything's better with gingersnaps," I say, but the truth is…

He tucks a lock of hair behind my ear before saying exactly what I was thinking.

"Everything's better with you."

Eight months later...

"ARE you sure you don't need any help?" I ask Julian.

"You're the birthday girl," he says, giving me a peck on the cheek before opening the fridge. "You're not supposed to do any work."

I head to the living room and wait for our guests to arrive.

There's a birthday party for me tonight at Julian's penthouse. Well, *our* penthouse, I guess, since I recently moved in. Julian is cooking—I don't know what, though I keep asking questions—and our families will be here at six. Yes, both of our families. This will be the first time our parents meet.

The last eight months haven't been perfect, but they were better than the previous three times I was depressed. I think it's over now —it was shorter than the other episodes. Julian and I went for a long walk yesterday. We passed by a garden, and when I saw the tulips, I just wanted to smile and enjoy their beauty. I no longer feel like I'm moving through molasses and seeing things through a thick fog. Now, everything seems bright and colorful and *alive*.

I didn't have to take leave from work, so that was an improvement. There were several rough days at the lab, but I made it through, and I've started being interested in my research again. I had some therapy sessions with a few different psychologists and finally found one I like. I think that may have helped me improve faster than the other times. Being in love and having a better support network were helpful, too.

Love can't cure my depression, but my relationship with Julian has enriched my life and made it easier to deal with the difficult times.

I look at the promise ring and smile.

Naomi and Will are the first to arrive. My sister and I had a good trip to New York City back in October. I didn't enjoy it as much as I would have if I hadn't been depressed, but it was helpful for me to have a break from my regular life. Naomi's financial situation is better now, and she moved in with Will a few months ago.

Jeremy, Lydia, and Heather are next. Heather is ten months old. She recently started crawling and likes to get into all sorts of trouble. Today, she's wearing a sailor dress.

"Look at you!" I say, taking her from Jeremy's arms. "Aren't you cute?"

She smiles at me. She's got a few teeth now.

One day, I will have this, too. I never thought it would be possible, but it is. And, yes, Julian and I have talked about it, and he is on board with the plan.

Julian's parents and grandmother arrive a few minutes later.

His grandmother looks at the baby in my arms. "You must have a baby of your own soon. I'm ninety now. Might not have much time." She pats my shoulder, then fingers the sleeve of my floral-print dress. "Very nice. You have big seduction plans after everyone leaves?"

"Ma!" exclaims Julian's mother.

"What? Courtney and I are having a serious conversation. No interrupting."

I'm glad my parents weren't here for that exchange.

Julian's mom shakes her head. "It's lovely to see you, Courtney. You look well."

His family knows about my problems. I didn't want to tell them at first, but in the end, I figured it would be easier. I was a little surprised the world didn't come crashing down around me when they found out.

Vince arrives next, carrying a bottle of wine.

"I'm surprised you didn't hire a clown," I say. "Or a petting zoo. Julian told me about your ideas."

Heather, who is now sitting in Lydia's lap, perks up at the words "petting zoo," though I don't think she understands what we're talking about.

"No," Vince says, "just the best wine for my sister. It's the one you liked the other night."

"I'm not your sister," I protest.

"Aw, come on. We know you will be soon."

This is true. I give him a smile.

Cedric arrives with another bottle of wine, and my parents are last. They look around the penthouse like they're in a museum. They've only been here once before, and they still can't believe I'm dating Julian Fong. Of course, they love him and fawn all over him to a rather embarrassing degree.

My parents aren't the biggest supports in my life, but unlike the previous few times I was unwell, we didn't fight on a regular basis. My father never snapped and said it was all in my head. It was a relief not to have to worry about what they would say to me.

I introduce my parents to Julian's parents. They immediately start talking about wedding plans—go figure—and grandchildren. Charles Fong says some nice things to my parents about how they raised a wonderful daughter, and I can feel my cheeks turning pink. My parents beam at me. I'm sure they never imagined Charles Fong talking about their daughter like this. They tell him how the Toronto Chinese-Canadian Center helped them when they first moved to Canada.

I return to the kitchen, where Julian is putting the finishing touches on a green salad with fresh figs and goat cheese. My heart swells at the sight of him.

"How's it going out there?" he asks. "Any fights yet?"

He's joking. Neither of us anticipate any problems.

He sweeps me into his arms. "I don't think anyone will mind if we take a minute to do this."

As he kisses me on the lips, I wonder if anyone will miss us if we head to the bedroom for five minutes and—

"I knew it!" says a high-pitched voice. "You had seduction plans."

"Po Po," Julian says, "you're not supposed to be anywhere near the kitchen tonight. Go out there and enjoy yourself."

"I did not come into kitchen to cook the whole meal. Just to make sure you know what you're doing."

"I know what I'm doing, I promise," he says, then winks at me. "I've done lots of cooking lately."

Vince walks into the kitchen. "What's going on in here? Am I missing all the fun? Is there a petting zoo after all?"

Julian, his arms still around me, shoots him a glare.

His grandmother takes Vince's hand. "We will go now. It's getting hot in here."

Vince, however, is unable to leave because he's doubled over in laughter.

When we're alone again, Julian brushes the hair back from my face and gives me one final kiss on the lips. "I suppose I should get back to cooking dinner."

"I suppose you should," I say, reluctant to leave.

When I look at him, all I can do is grin. A year ago, I never would have imagined having a happy thirty-second birthday dinner with a boyfriend and our families.

I still have my struggles, and my life isn't perfect.

But I wouldn't trade it for anything.

JULIAN

I cooked a great leg of lamb, if I do say so myself, and Courtney practically drooled when she saw the chocolate-raspberry cake I made. It tasted as good as it looked, too.

We had sex after everyone left. Now she's sleeping, her head resting on my shoulder, and I'm stroking her hair. I still can't get over how beautiful she is, and she's *mine*.

My life used to be a non-stop cycle of work, but I was missing out on so much—as she's shown me. Now I have a good balance of business and pleasure, and I'm in no danger of burning out. I do things like bake lemon squares for no particular reason and read on my rooftop patio with a bottle of "old man" beer and a novel. What's the point of having a rooftop patio and gorgeous views of the city if you never take the time to enjoy them? Courtney particularly likes when I read shirtless on the patio, though I never seem to get much reading done when she's up there with me. Strange how that happens.

In the past few weeks, I've also done some scrapbooking in secret. I have another surprise—and another ring—to give her when we go back to Montreal for Canada Day weekend.

I know she'll say yes.

The terrarium is doing well. Joey the Cactus is doing well. He's started growing toward the light, and he's a little less…erect than he was before.

But enough about cacti.

My father is enjoying being back at work part-time, and Mom

is thrilled he's stopped his amateur efforts at carpentry. Raymond is now president of Fong Investments, and he's taken over some of my responsibilities. Po Po has yet to play Chinese opera at my office.

Courtney is well now, too. There were a few difficult months, but at no point did I ever think of leaving her. I'm glad she, too, had faith I would always be there.

She's the most important part of my life, and she's changed me for the better. Somehow, my impulsive decision to give her five thousand dollars to teach me how to have fun turned into something truly amazing.

"I love you," I murmur.

She doesn't open her eyes, but she mumbles, "I love you, too."

Yes, sometimes I do important things at work that involve great sums of money, but the best moments in my life are moments like these, when I get to hold the woman I love.

I turn out the light and settle my head on the pillow, right next to Courtney.

I wouldn't trade this for anything.

ACKNOWLEDGMENTS

Thank you to Farah Heron for beta reading the manuscript, and to my editor, Latoya C. Smith, for helping me make this book the best it could be. Thank you also to Toronto Romance Writers, as well as my husband and father, for all your support.

ABOUT THE AUTHOR

Jackie Lau decided she wanted to be a writer when she was in grade two, sometime between writing "The Heart That Got Lost" and "The Land of Shapes." She later studied engineering and worked as a geophysicist before turning to writing romance novels. Jackie lives in Toronto with her husband, and despite living in Canada her whole life, she hates winter. When she's not writing, she enjoys gelato, gourmet donuts, cooking, hiking, and reading on the balcony when it's raining.

To learn more and sign up for her newsletter, visit jackielaubooks.com.

CPSIA information can be obtained
at www.ICGtesting.com
Printed in the USA
LVHW091518011119
636084LV00001B/112/P